With a knowing smile, the tarot reader walked over to Prue, Piper, and Phoebe's table. "I am Elena. You wish me to look into your future with my cards?"

This is going to be a joke, Prue told herself as Elena laid down the first card.

Elena's hand began to tremble. Prue jerked her gaze to the fortune-teller's face. It grew pale, a ghostly white, as though all the blood had been drained from it.

"What is it?" Prue asked, trying to ignore the irrational prickle of dread that was raising the hair on the nape of her neck.

"Th-this card has always been in the deck, but I've never drawn it during a reading," Elena stammered. She set it on the table, and Prue saw that it showed a crumbling black tower struck by lightning.

"What does it mean?" Prue asked.

Elena trembled again. "It is the most powerful card in the deck," she said slowly, her voice an ominous whisper. "It means that darkness will surround you."

Charmed™

The Power of Three
By Eliza Willard

Kiss of Darkness
By Brandon Alexander

Pocket Pulse
Published by Pocket Books

For orders other than by individual consumers, Pocket Books grants a discount on the purchase of **10 or more** copies of single titles for special markets or premium use. For further details, please write to the Vice President of Special Markets, Pocket Books, 1230 Avenue of the Americas, 9th Floor, New York, NY 10020-1586.

For information on how individual consumers can place orders, please write to Mail Order Department, Simon & Schuster Inc., 100 Front Street, Riverside, NJ 08075.

KISS OF DARKNESS

An original novel by Brandon Alexander
Based on the hit TV series *Charmed*,
Created by Constance M. Burge

A Parachute Press Book

POCKET PULSE

New York London Toronto Sydney Singapore

This book is a work of fiction. Names, characters, places and incidents are products of the author's imagination or are used fictitiously. Any resemblance to actual events or locales or persons, living or dead, is entirely coincidental.

An *Original* Publication of POCKET BOOKS

POCKET PULSE published by
Pocket Books, a division of Simon & Schuster Inc.
1230 Avenue of the Americas, New York, NY 10020

TM & © 2000 Spelling Television Inc. All Rights Reserved.

ISBN: 0-671-04163-0

First Pocket Pulse printing February 2000

10 9 8 7 6 5 4 3 2 1

POCKET PULSE and colophon are trademarks of Simon & Schuster Inc.

Printed in the U.S.A.

CHAPTER
1

I still can't believe this year went so fast," Prue Halliwell told her younger sisters as they ate lunch at the Railyard Café, a restaurant near her job at Buckland's Auction House. "I mean, it's New Year's Eve already! How did *that* happen?"

Twenty-five-year-old Piper cleared her throat. "Well, last year was kind of . . . intense, if you know what I mean."

"Tell me about it," Phoebe added.

Prue sipped her iced tea. They're right, she thought. Last year was definitely a year of changes. Grams passed away and left us Halliwell Manor, the house we were raised in. Then Piper and I moved back into the old Victorian, and Phoebe came home from New York City to move in with us.

But Prue knew that it was what Phoebe had

1

discovered in the attic that forced the biggest change in their lives.

Phoebe found *The Book of Shadows*—an ancient text of witchcraft—and read an incantation from it. It was an incantation that awakened powers we never knew we had, Prue thought, and made us realize we weren't like everybody else.

We're the Charmed Ones—the most powerful witches, dedicated to protecting the innocent and fighting off evil warlocks and demons. Prue took a deep breath. It was a lot to swallow.

She pushed her dark, bobbed hair behind her ears. "Hopefully this new year will be a little less eventful for us," she told her sisters.

"Speak for yourself," Phoebe said. "I need a little action in my life. And I'm not starting things off on the right foot."

"So, you're trying to say *what?*" Piper asked her.

"Tonight," Phoebe replied. "It's New Year's Eve and I don't even have a date." She propped her chin on her hand and gave her sisters a mournful look.

Piper shook back her long brown hair and shrugged. "So? I don't have one either. It's not the end of the world."

"It's different for you. You manage the hottest restaurant in San Francisco, and you're hosting the ultimate New Year's Eve party," Phoebe pointed out. "Quake will be so busy tonight that you won't even notice that you don't have a date."

"Trust me," Piper replied. "I'll notice."

Prue took a bite of her grilled salmon. "Okay," she admitted. "We've all been pretty dateless lately, but that gives us time to concentrate on other things—like our careers. I think that's a good thing."

Phoebe laughed. "That's because you're extremely strange."

"Me?" Prue arched a dark eyebrow. "In case you haven't noticed, ever since you found *The Book of Shadows* a lot of things in our lives have been more than strange."

"Come on," Phoebe said. "I did you a favor. How many women do you know who can move things with their minds?"

"That's the whole point," Prue replied. "It's a little hard to have a relationship with a guy when you're"— she looked around the crowded restaurant, then leaned in closer to her sisters—"a witch," she whispered.

Phoebe's brown eyes widened. "That doesn't mean we have to give up on dating and start collecting cats," she said. "I don't want to be an old maid."

Prue tried hard not to laugh at Phoebe. The three Halliwell sisters had all lucked into large eyes, great cheekbones, straight, silky hair, and extremely nice figures. "At twenty-two, Phoebe, I highly doubt anyone would ever call you an old maid."

"You know what I mean," Phoebe insisted. "Besides, what good is having special powers when they can't even get you a date for New Year's Eve?"

"She's got a point," Piper agreed as she stirred her soup. "But you know the rules. We can't use our powers for personal gain. We can use them only to—"

"I know, I know—to protect the innocent," Phoebe finished. "Still," she continued in a dreamy tone, "I keep hoping I'll have a vision of me and some outrageously gorgeous guy in a total lip-lock just as the clock strikes twelve." She looked hopefully at Piper. "Actually that drummer for the Night Owls would do. You were so lucky to get that band to play at Quake tonight. They're going to make it big someday."

Prue glanced up, intrigued by Phoebe's confidence in the band. "Premonition?" she asked.

Phoebe rolled her eyes. "Can't you give me credit for knowing some things on my own without tapping into my power? I know talent when I hear it. And the guys are all incredibly cute. *Especially* the drummer."

"I wish you were going to be at Quake's party, Prue," Piper said. "It won't feel like New Year's without you."

"I'll be there," Prue assured her. She knew it meant a lot to Piper. "I just have to put in an appearance at Lloyd Claiborne's party first."

"Rough life," Phoebe told Prue. "Going to a party at one of the most elegant mansions in Pacific Heights, rubbing elbows with the rich and famous . . ."

"Yeah, too bad it's for work," Prue said. "Lloyd Claiborne is one of Buckland's biggest clients and one of the most important collectors in the city. He's invited all the appraisers at the auction house. My boss, Claire, made it clear that we're all supposed to show. She doesn't want to risk offending him."

"I wonder what kind of food he's going to serve," Piper mused. "I'm guessing Pacific Rim and totally gourmet."

"Giovanni's is catering the event," Prue told her.

"Oh, that's classic Italian. But it figures. Only the most exclusive restaurant in the city."

"I wish you could both come," Prue said, meaning it. "It's not as much fun going to parties alone."

"You *will* try to come to Quake's party later though, right?" Piper asked.

Prue nodded. "I said I would. Probably not until after midnight, but I promise I'll show."

"Oooh," Phoebe whispered as her gaze slid past Prue. "Piper, we need to have *him* at Quake tonight. Do you have any of those flyers on you? I want to make sure this guy gets one."

Prue glanced over her shoulder. Her breath caught, and she knew immediately which man Phoebe was talking about. Tall, with gleaming black hair and mesmerizing blue eyes, the man strode toward their table.

"Don't invite him," Prue ordered in a low voice.

"Are you kidding? He's gorgeous," Piper whispered.

"Don't, please," Prue repeated.

The man stopped before her, took her hand, and brought it to his lips. "Hello, Prue. It's been too long since we've seen each other. I've been thinking about you."

Prue tried to ignore the man's charming French accent and the shivers it sent skittering up her spine. She withdrew her hand from his. "It hasn't been that long."

"Two hundred and eighty-five nights," the man said quietly.

Prue stared at him. "You counted the nights?"

"I was trying to impress you." He grinned. "Will you be at Claiborne's party this evening?" he asked.

Prue nodded. "I'll be there."

He tilted his head slightly. "Then I'll look forward to midnight."

"Midnight," Prue repeated. She knew he was hinting at a kiss, something she'd have a hard time resisting. But it might lead to something more, and that was definitely a place she was not ready to go. "I'm not into these New Year's Eve rituals of kissing men I barely know," she warned him.

"That's a shame." The man looked anything but discouraged. In fact, he seemed intrigued by the challenge. "Maybe we'll have a chance to at least talk. Until later, then. Take care, Prue."

He left the restaurant, and Prue breathed a sigh of relief. It would have been so easy just to invite him to go to the Claiborne party with her.

"Who was *that?*" Piper asked as soon as the man was out of sight.

"His name is Robert Galliard," Prue explained. "He's a Parisian antiques dealer who spends a couple of months in San Francisco every winter. We met last year."

"Why did you give him the freeze treatment?" Phoebe demanded.

"Phoebe, *I'm* the one with the power to freeze time, remember?" Piper said with a goofy smile.

Prue groaned. "Bad, Piper. Really, really bad."

"Back to the subject at hand, Prue," Phoebe continued. "That guy is gorgeous, he's got a sexy French accent, and he's into antiques, which, I should point out, also happens to be one of your major obsessions. And you acted like an ice queen."

Prue sighed, remembering last winter when she first met Robert. They flirted, discussed eighteenth-century French jewelry and Ming vases. They even wound up at the same museum show together. She kept expecting him to ask her out, but he didn't. Then he returned to Paris.

But now he's back, Prue thought, and I can tell he's ready to get involved. But my world has changed dramatically since we met each other.

"I didn't give him the freeze treatment," she explained to her sisters. "I just don't want to encourage him. I mean, I think he's interested in me—"

"*Think?*" Piper interrupted. "How about 'no doubt about it'? Prue, he didn't have to come over here to talk to you."

"And he didn't have to kiss your hand,"

Phoebe pointed out. She batted her eyelashes. "That was so sweet."

"I know he's handsome and charming, but after Piper's experience—"

"You think he's a warlock?" Piper asked, wincing.

Prue knew that her sister hadn't quite recovered from dating Jeremy Burns. She'd been crazy about him—only to discover he was a warlock who wanted the Charmed Ones dead.

"You never know," Prue answered. "Also, dating is not something I think I can handle right now."

"You mean, you don't think Robert can accept the fact that you're a witch," Phoebe added.

"I don't know," Prue admitted, staring at the straw in her iced tea. "I just know that these powers are still new to us. And until I'm comfortable with who I am, I'm swearing off men for a while. Besides, I told you. I want to concentrate on my career."

"Oh, that makes sense," Phoebe said. "Cataloguing musty old relics is much more fun than going out with a gorgeous Frenchman."

"It's scary taking a risk with your heart, and it hurts when it doesn't work out," Prue said in a quiet voice. "I just don't know how any guy will feel when he discovers I'm a witch. You have to have honesty in a relationship, not secrets. So for now, dealing with antiques seems simpler—and a lot safer."

Piper gave Prue a sympathetic smile. "Understood. But someday we're all going to have to take that chance."

"Maybe *she* can tell us when," Phoebe said, nodding to a young woman talking to a couple at a nearby table.

Prue shifted in her chair slightly and saw the young woman Phoebe was motioning toward. She was wearing a skirt made of colored scarves sewn together in a patchwork pattern. Her flame-red hair flowed across still more scarves that draped over her shoulders, wrapped around her body, and tucked into a wide sash at her waist. Silver rings set with large stones adorned her fingers, and heavy silver bracelets clanked against her wrists. Even from a distance, Prue knew enough about antiques to know the jewelry was ancient.

The red-haired woman began to lay cards on a nearby table occupied by a young couple.

"She's giving a tarot reading," Piper whispered.

"You should get one, Prue. To know if you should concentrate on your career or on Robert," Phoebe teased.

Prue glared at her sisters. "I know what I need to concentrate on—"

"Let's all get a reading," Phoebe suggested. "What better time than the last day of the year to find out what the future holds?"

"Give me a break. Tarot reading is a cheap trick," Prue said. "She tells you something vague, and then, when something happens, you think 'Oh, that's what the cards meant.' "

"And witches don't exist except in fairy tales," Phoebe added. "Let's do it. Just for fun. You don't have to believe in it."

"I don't want to do this," Prue said, feeling a foreboding that she couldn't explain. She knew only that she didn't want anyone telling her what would happen to her. She'd never envied Phoebe's ability to see glimpses of the future.

"Oh, come on, Prue," Piper urged her. "We'll all do it."

"Pretty please?" Phoebe smiled.

Prue gave a sigh of resignation. Her sisters were not about to let go of this idea. "All right," she agreed.

Holding her cards, the tarot reader rose from the table, and her glance went directly to Prue.

Prue felt an icy shiver race along her spine. Her reaction made no sense. The woman wasn't threatening her.

With a knowing smile, the tarot reader walked over to their table. "I am Elena. You wish me to look into your future with my cards? It is five dollars each."

Prue started to reach into her purse. Phoebe grabbed her hand. "It was my idea. I'll pay."

"With what?" Prue asked, staring at her. Her sister had yet to find a job or decide what she wanted to do with her life. She never had enough money for herself, let alone extra for treating her sisters.

Phoebe grimaced. "Right. I didn't bring my bag."

"I convinced Prue to do it, so I'll treat," Piper told them.

"No argument there," Prue said as Piper dug some money out of her purse.

Piper handed fifteen dollars to Elena. Prue watched her slip it between her scarves, no doubt into a hidden pocket.

"I'll start with the one who paid," Elena said. She began to lay the tarot cards on the table in front of Piper in a pattern that resembled a cross.

Prue had seen tarot cards before. Old European decks sometimes came through the auction house. And this deck was definitely old—the colors in the images were faded and the corners of the cards were cracked with use. But it was different from other decks she'd seen. She didn't recognize the traditional minor and major arcana. There were some images that seemed familiar—a court jester or fool, a king, an old man with a beard—but many more that weren't.

"What kind of deck is this?" Prue asked, curious.

Elena shrugged. "A fortune-teller's deck. The cards reveal the future."

"Right," Prue said. "But that's not what I meant. I work with antiques, so I'm curious about the deck's history."

"The cards are very old," Elena said as she continued to slowly lay them in front of Piper. "For generations, within my family, they have been passed from mother to daughter," Elena went on.

"How many generations?" Prue asked, skeptical but still intrigued.

"Too many to count," Elena replied.

Prue watched Elena smile at Piper after she laid down the final card.

"Ah," Elena murmured. "It is your time to be noticed."

Piper grinned. "Me? The dateless wonder? That's a nice change."

"Your life is indeed changing. In the future—the near future—many will notice you," Elena assured her. She gathered up her cards and turned to Phoebe. "Are you ready?"

"As ready as I'll ever be," Phoebe said.

Prue leaned forward as Elena laid out the cards for Phoebe. Though the cards were faded, they were beautiful—edged in silver and gold and illustrated with highly detailed images. Prue tried to fix the border design into her memory; maybe she could find some information about this particular deck when she returned to her office. "Where does the deck come from?" she asked.

"Somewhere in France," Elena answered, never taking her eyes off the cards. "It was always whispered in my family that one of our ancestors, a man who practiced the Dark Arts, created the cards. He taught his daughter how to read them, and the knowledge has been passed down through the centuries."

Phoebe went a little pale. "The Dark Arts? Maybe we shouldn't be messing with something created by a guy who was into the Dark Arts."

Elena's eyes held hers. "The cards themselves

are neither good nor bad. What matters is the intention of the one who reads them."

"And your intention is . . . ?" Piper asked.

"To tell the future, to entertain you, and to make my living," Elena replied smoothly. She smiled at Phoebe. "You will come into money."

Phoebe grinned. "That's *exactly* what I wanted to hear."

What a coincidence, Prue thought. The reader was such a fake. Hadn't they hinted at Phoebe's lack of money almost as soon as Elena came to the table? It didn't take tarot cards to make that prediction.

Elena turned to Prue. "And now you."

This is going to be a joke, Prue told herself as Elena laid down the first card. It was the jester, which probably meant that she was a fool for agreeing to this in the first place.

Elena drew a second card from the deck.

Prue watched in fascination as Elena's hand began to tremble. She jerked her gaze to the fortune-teller's face. It grew pale, a ghostly white, as though all the blood had been drained from it.

"What is it?" Prue asked, trying to ignore the irrational prickle of dread that was raising the hair on the nape of her neck.

"Th-this card has always been in the deck, but I've never drawn it during a reading," Elena stammered. She set it on the table, and Prue saw that it showed a crumbling black tower struck by lightning.

"What does it mean?" Prue asked.

Elena quickly returned the card to the deck. "It was a mistake," she said, and set down another card, this one showing a man and woman embracing. "For you I see romance and . . . and that is all."

"You saw more than romance," Prue insisted, disturbed by the fortune-teller's reaction. "Tell me the truth."

Elena trembled again. She set the card back down in front of Prue. "It is the most powerful card in the deck," she said slowly, her voice an ominous whisper. "It means that darkness will surround you."

CHAPTER 2

Darkness?" Prue laughed. "You can't exactly go wrong with that prediction, can you? As soon as the sun goes down, it'll be night and I'll be surrounded by darkness."

"It is not a natural darkness," Elena said, a tremor in her voice.

"What kind of darkness is it, then?" Prue asked, picking up the card.

"You shouldn't touch it," Elena snapped, reaching for the card. "Only the owner of the deck should handle the cards."

Prue pulled the card beyond the woman's reach and studied it closely. Oddly, unlike the others in the deck, this card had not faded. Its background was a deep, rich emerald green. In its center, bolts of silver lightning sliced through a black tower. The sky around the tower was filled with strange geometric symbols.

Prue had seen a lot of weird things lately. Since learning of her true heritage, she was growing accustomed to things—and people—not being exactly what they appeared to be. So why, she wondered, did this card make her so uneasy?

Narrowing her eyes, she met Elena's gaze. "Tell me exactly what the tower and all these symbols mean."

Elena smiled and held out her open palm, her hand no longer trembling. "I'll explain for ten more dollars."

That, I could have predicted, Prue thought. She dropped the card on the table. "Thanks, but no thanks. I don't need to start off the new year with a scam."

Elena's face flushed red. "You will pay a higher price later if you don't pay the smaller price now," she warned.

Shaking her head in disbelief at the woman's nerve, Prue laughed lightly. "I'll take my chances."

Standing near the band, Piper swayed in rhythm to the pumping music of the Night Owls. This party is amazing, she thought, watching the restaurant's guests go wild on the dance floor.

Someday the Night Owls will be on every radio station in the country, she thought, and I'll be able to say that they'd played at Quake on New Year's Eve.

Piper gazed around the restaurant, thrilled to see it so packed. It was wall-to-wall party, and the crowd was incredible. The place looked as though it had been invaded by supermodels. Even the guys were better looking than usual. Maybe it's because everyone's dressed up, she thought as she caught a glimpse of Matt, one of the restaurant's regulars.

Piper scanned the room, and spotted Phoebe dancing with a guy with blond dreadlocks. Piper laughed. He was probably the twentieth guy her sister had danced with so far.

I don't know why she was complaining earlier. Phoebe has no trouble getting men, Piper thought. I wish I could meet guys that easily.

Then again, Phoebe was wearing a super-short and slinky black dress. She was hard to ignore. Piper thought of Elena's tarot reading and decided that the fortune-teller was wrong. It was Phoebe who was getting noticed. As usual.

"Piper." One of the waiters came up to her. "Billy's getting a little backlogged in the kitchen. I think he needs help."

"I'm on it." She turned toward the kitchen to rescue her assistant chef—and came to a sudden stop. A guy sitting alone at a table on the edge of the dance floor was watching her. His incredible brown eyes locked onto hers, and she felt the breath back up in her lungs.

Even though she'd complained about not having a boyfriend, like Prue, Piper wasn't sure she was ready to get involved with anyone. But this guy was so cute. His blond hair fell across his forehead. She watched him comb it back with his fingers, a grin tugging up one corner of his mouth.

She thought about asking him if his meal was all right. Instead, she averted her gaze and hurried toward the kitchen. She couldn't help but remember what a disaster Jeremy had been. How were she and her sisters supposed to know who was safe?

Piper was a few feet from the kitchen door when Phoebe intercepted her. Phoebe's dark eyes were shining. "You did it!"

"Did what?" Piper asked.

"This! It's got to be the hottest party in the entire city! I told you the Night Owls would be incredible!"

"You did," Piper admitted happily.

"And the guys," Phoebe went on. "I have never seen this many exceptional-looking guys in one place. Not to mention guys who can actually dance." Wrapping her hand around Piper's arm, Phoebe asked, "What do you think of that blond one sitting at the table by the dance floor?"

Gorgeous was the word that came to Piper's mind. "I just noticed him," she confessed. "I've never seen him in here before, but . . . it kind of looked like he was watching me."

"He was definitely watching you," Phoebe assured her. "So I've had my sisterly eye on him, and I'm happy to report that it doesn't look like he's with anyone."

Piper suddenly got a bad case of the nerves that made her feel as if she were thirteen and a complete social misfit all over again.

Phoebe nudged her shoulder. "Go ask him his name."

Piper widened her eyes. "Are you crazy? I can't do that."

"Why not?"

"Because," Piper said, resigned, "I'm not you. I can't just go up to someone." She shook her head. "I don't even know him."

Phoebe leaned closer. "That's why you have to go talk to him. So you can *get* to know him."

Piper took a deep breath to calm her nerves. She really *did* want to know who he was. For that brief moment when their eyes had met, she'd felt a connection with him. But talking to men she didn't know was not her style. "I wouldn't know what to say."

"Piper, there is a time to be shy and a time to be bold. This is New Year's Eve—" She paused. "All right. You're the manager. You can introduce yourself and tell him that you're taking a random survey to see if everyone is having a good time."

Piper stared at her sister. "That is so lame. I can't say *that*. Look, I'm not going up to him, okay? That's it."

Phoebe glared at her. "Hypocrite."

Piper's mouth dropped open. "I am not—"

"This afternoon you agreed with me that Prue shouldn't let that incredible guy walk out of her life, and now you won't walk over to a good-looking guy and let him into *your* life. That makes you a hypocrite."

Piper growled low in her throat. She hated it when Phoebe was right. And she knew Phoebe would harp on this for the rest of the night. "Oh, all right. Anything to stop your nagging."

Piper studied the guy more closely. He was so beautiful. She squared her shoulders. "Okay. I'm just going to walk over there and make sure his food is okay."

Phoebe patted her back. "That-a-girl. Don't forget to ask his name, give him yours, and maybe shove your phone number under his nose."

"Phoebe," Piper warned.

Phoebe held up her hands. "Just kidding. I won't even watch. I'm going by the band to flirt with the drummer."

Piper watched Phoebe head toward the dance floor. She took a slow, calming breath. You can do this, she told herself.

Passing waiters carrying trays filled with hors d'oeuvres and champagne glasses, she started toward his table. His hair was so blond. He turned his attention away from the band, and his gaze met hers. He had incredible brown eyes.

Piper gasped. I can't do it. She turned quickly—and collided with a waiter holding a full tray of champagne. She shrieked as a cascading waterfall of sparkling wine poured over her. Then she shut her eyes as she heard the glasses shatter against the floor.

"Gravity check!" someone yelled.

Everyone in the restaurant began to laugh and applaud.

Piper felt the chilled champagne soak into her dress. The wet feeling was completely uncomfortable, and her dress was ruined. But that was nothing compared to the fact that she was dying a slow death by humiliation. She wished she could have used her power to freeze time to prevent it, but the accident had happened too fast.

"I'm so sorry, Piper," the waiter said. "I didn't expect you to turn around so fast."

She shook her head. "It's all right, Danny."

"I'll get this cleaned up," he promised as he dropped to his knees, grabbed the tray, and began to pick up the broken glass.

"Let me help you," Piper said, kneeling beside him.

A warm hand wrapped around her arm. "Are you all right?"

Piper looked in the direction of the concerned voice. It was him! She stared into the warm brown eyes of the man who had been sitting by the dance floor, the guy she'd planned to introduce herself to. He gave her a friendly smile, and her mortification factor increased by ten. "I'm . . . I'm fine," she stammered. "Just covered in wine."

"So you're a poet," he teased.

Fine? Wine? Piper wanted to scream. "No, I'm an idiot," she told him. She wanted to escape as quickly as possible. "I've . . . got to . . . go check on Billy."

"Who's Billy?" he asked, seeming disappointed. "Your boyfriend?"

Piper gasped. "No, uh, not at all. He's my assistant chef."

"So you're the one responsible for this great party?"

She glanced down at her soaked dress, then lifted her gaze back to his. "I'm responsible for the party, the spilled champagne, the broken glasses. All of it," she confessed miserably. Then out of nowhere she heard herself blurt out, "Is your food okay?"

His grin grew. "My food is fine."

"Great. That's all I wanted to know." It was definitely not the time to offer him her name or phone number. What was she supposed to do? Hand him her card and say, "Here. Want to go out with a klutz? Call Piper."

"I—I've really got to go," she told him, and turned to flee.

"Wait. Please. Don't go yet," the guy said, gently touching her arm again.

Piper froze. She slowly turned back to face him.

"I've been trying to figure out a way to talk to you all night," he said, glancing at his shoes, then back at her.

"Really?" Piper felt her heart tighten. Maybe she wasn't the only shy one there tonight.

He gave her self-conscious grin. "Yeah, really. I'm Jake Stone."

She smiled softly. "Piper Halliwell."

"Piper. That's an unusual name. I like it."

"It was my mother's idea."

He laughed. She liked the sound.

"Names usually are a mother's idea," Jake said. "I guess you need to get back to Billy."

"Billy?" she asked.

He grinned at her. "Your assistant chef."

"Oh, Billy. Right." She touched her wet dress. "And I need to change, too."

He pointed toward his table. "You know where to find me."

Smiling brightly, she headed toward her office. Oh, yes, she knew where to find him, and more important, she knew he *wanted* her to find him.

Prue felt as though she'd walked into a dream. The guest list for Lloyd Claiborne's party was a Who's Who of San Francisco's elite. Prue had been there for only half an hour, and already she'd been introduced to the mayor, a soloist from the city ballet, the owner of a Sonoma vineyard, the heir to an oil fortune, the head of a giant Internet company, a film producer, and the director of the modern art museum. It was—to put it mildly—a little overwhelming.

A chamber orchestra played in the ballroom, and waiters moved through the crowd, offering hors d'oeuvres and glasses of wine and champagne. But for Prue the most impressive thing was the mansion itself, which felt like a private museum filled with priceless antiques and works of art.

On either side of the huge foyer, wide, curving

stairs swept up to the second floor. She had taken
her time exploring, starting with the first-floor
rooms, where she'd admired contemporary
sculptures, a Louis XIV desk, French Renaissance
tapestries, a fountain from an Italian villa, and
Persian silk rugs.

Then she'd ascended the stairs, where a mezzanine linked the two sets of steps and led to the
east and west wings of the house. Prue decided to
explore the second floor later. Instead, she took
the single marble stairway that rose from the
mezzanine to the third floor and a wall of French
doors that opened onto a wrought-iron balcony.
Prue stepped onto the balcony, dazzled by the
view. The lights of the Golden Gate Bridge glim-
mered in the distance.

"Beautiful view, isn't it?" a male voice asked.

She turned and smiled at Lloyd Claiborne. He
was perhaps ten years older than she was, with a
bit of silver hair at his temples. She knew he'd in-
herited his wealth; still, it was hard not to feel a
little awed by him.

"It's incredible," she admitted.

"Have you had the grand tour?" he asked.

She nodded. "Well, part of it. I haven't really
seen the second floor yet. Still . . . some of the
things you have here, I've seen only in art books."

Claiborne gave her a curious look, and Prue
cringed inwardly. Did I just sound like a total
amateur? she wondered. "What I mean," she
tried again, "is that it's a privilege to view your
collection."

"I've always thought it a shame to hide beautiful things," Claiborne said easily. "Especially from those who can truly appreciate them. I was impressed by the catalogue you wrote for the art deco glass auction," he explained. "I've given your name to a few of my friends who are interested in antiques."

Prue felt as though she'd just won a prize. "I'm honored that you would do that. Thank you."

"Well, to be quite honest with you, sometimes I find Claire a bit stuffy. Now, if you'll excuse me, I have more guests to welcome."

Prue watched Claiborne walk away, thinking he'd made this a night she would never forget. She was nearly floating on the sweet feeling of success.

Well, I guess that couldn't last, Prue thought a moment later as she spotted Claire walking toward her. Prue loved working in an auction house, but her boss was a different story. As usual, Claire wore a sour, pinched expression. Even at a party, Claire couldn't allow herself to have a good time.

"Prue," Claire said. She stood on the other side of the French doors, refusing to step out on the balcony. "What were you and Mr. Claiborne talking about?"

Prue stepped back inside. "Antiques," she answered, deadpan. She wished Claire would go away.

"What about them?" Claire persisted. "You didn't say anything to embarrass me, did you? Tell me the whole conversation."

"Claiborne said he was impressed with the art deco glass auction," Prue replied carefully. She knew that if she told Claire that Claiborne was impressed with her work, Claire would find some way to hold it against her. "He said he was going to send other clients our way."

Claire closed her eyes as though relieved. "Thank goodness." She opened her eyes. "You need to mingle and make more contacts. You're here to work, not have fun."

Prue had a strong urge to salute but she didn't. "I'll do my best," she said.

As soon as Claire walked away, Prue rolled her eyes. I hope I never get so obsessed with work that I can't have fun, she thought. Then she realized that was exactly what she'd told her sisters she'd planned to do—concentrate on her career and not even think about fun.

Prue suddenly wished she were at the Quake party, where her boss wasn't watching her every move.

She took a glass of champagne from a passing waiter and returned to the balcony. Fireworks exploded in streaks of gold and green over the water as she sipped her drink. A chill suddenly swept through her, sending shivers along the nape of her neck. She had the oddest sensation that someone was watching her. She whirled around.

Elena, the tarot reader, stood at the threshold to the balcony, her silvery eyes gleaming with triumph. "I was right, you see."

Prue's mouth dropped open. Something about the fortune-teller gave her the willies. She once again wore a dress made of scarves, but this time they were all black silk. "Wh-what are you doing here?" Prue stammered.

"Watching my prediction come true," Elena rattled off quickly before turning and rushing down the stairs, her scarves billowing out behind her.

How did she know where to find me? Prue wondered. Elena was only a table away from us at lunch. She might have overheard us talking, Prue realized. But that seemed improbable. Elena hadn't been paying any attention to the Halliwells until she'd come over to do their tarot readings. And now Elena being here—it was all too weird.

Prue stepped back into the house, welcoming the light from Claiborne's dazzling crystal chandelier. She shivered again, remembering Elena's creepy prediction: Surrounded by darkness. What does it mean? Prue wondered.

"Who was that?" someone asked.

Prue spun around at the deep voice and pressed her hand above her pounding heart. It was a man she'd never seen before, an elderly gentleman with thick white hair and an impeccably tailored tuxedo.

"She's someone I met this afternoon at the Railyard Café," Prue answered. "She gives tarot readings."

"Really? I'm surprised Lloyd invited her," he

said. "She looks a little eccentric for his usual guest list." The man held out his hand. "I'm Jason Roman. Lloyd told me you were the antiques expert."

Prue smiled as she shook his hand. "I work at Buckland's."

"Unfortunately I'm not much into antiques," he admitted, "but I do like a woman who is different from everyone else."

Prue felt her stomach knot up. Had he somehow guessed she was a witch? Though she knew that was impossible, she sometimes felt as though people could tell she had powers simply by looking at her. "Different?" she asked him.

Roman smiled. "Maybe you haven't noticed, but you're the only woman here not wearing black."

Prue glanced around quickly. Whether the other women were in sequins or silk, they were all wearing black. The men all wore black tuxedoes. Prue looked down at her bright red silk dress.

She met Jason's gaze and laughed lightly. "I supposed you could say that I'm surrounded by darkness."

He smiled. "You could indeed. Personally I find the red a welcome distraction." He lifted his champagne glass to toast her. "It makes you stand out in the crowd."

Prue nodded and lifted her glass too. "Thank you," she said, feeling as if she might collapse with relief. So much for worrying about Elena and her ridiculous predictions.

She bid farewell to Jason Roman, then descended the marble staircase. She handed her empty glass to a waiter and spotted Robert Galliard on the first floor, walking through the crowded foyer to shake hands with Lloyd Claiborne.

Then Robert's gaze shot to hers as though he knew exactly where to find her. A slow smile spread across his face, and he began climbing the stairs.

Prue was surprised that she was so glad to see him. She'd met several men at the party, and had even talked with a few about the significance of Claiborne's collection, but no one had appreciated the rare treasures the way she knew Robert would.

Phoebe was right, Prue realized. She and Robert had a lot in common. Unfortunately there was still the little problem of the Halliwells' family secret. She wondered if her father knew he had married a witch. After all, her mother had never mentioned that fact to her daughters. Will part of my life always be secret? Prue wondered.

Unfortunately *The Book of Shadows* didn't come with guidelines or instructions on proper witch etiquette—only spells, incantations, and short history lessons on evil creatures that haunted the night.

Robert reached the top of the stairs and walked up to her. "Hello," he said in his rich French accent.

Prue did find the way he pronounced words

charming. She wanted to know him better, and yet she was afraid of where that might lead. "You missed the fireworks," she replied, trying to keep her voice light.

"I got caught in traffic. I was worried that I might miss you too." He looked at her intently, his blue eyes drawing her in until she felt she could easily drown in them.

As he took her hand, warm shivers traveled up her arm. Prue couldn't help wishing she were ready to get involved. But she wasn't, and it was better not to let things even get started. "Actually I was just about to leave," she said.

Robert's eyes widened in disbelief. "What is the point in coming to a New Year's Eve party if you leave before midnight?"

"Curiosity. From the day I started work at Buckland's, I've been hearing about Lloyd Claiborne's house and collection. I couldn't turn down an invitation to see them for myself. Besides," she confessed, "Claire made it clear that she considered this a command performance for all the appraisers."

"Yes, Claire would," he agreed with a smile. "But you're right about the collection. It is one of the finest in your country. Especially since"—he gave her a look of mock modesty—"I sold him several pieces myself. And Claire does have a point. The better you know your customer, the easier it is to sell him what he wants."

As a waiter passed by, Robert reached out and took two flutes of champagne from the tray. He handed one to Prue. "Please stay a little longer."

Prue smiled. "I'll stay until this glass of champagne is empty. I promised my sisters that I'd meet them at Quake."

"Quake?" he asked.

Prue nodded. "It's the restaurant my sister Piper manages. They're supposed to have an amazing band tonight."

"Then I will go with you," Robert offered. "Claiborne's chamber orchestra is elegant but not anything you can dance to."

Why am I fighting it? Prue asked herself. Robert is charming, gorgeous, and one of the few men I've met who actually cares about antiques. Reluctantly she gave in and nodded. "All right, but it's a very different kind of party."

She watched his eyes light with satisfaction at her acceptance, then become curious.

"Were you having lunch with your sister when I saw you today?" he asked.

"Yes. Actually with both my sisters. I'm sorry. I was rude not to introduce you."

"You can introduce me at Quake." He clinked his glass against hers. "Let us forget the past."

Prue smiled. "But the past is what we specialize in."

Robert glanced around the house. "Claiborne's mansion reminds me of a museum," he said.

"Me too. Can you imagine living in it?"

"I like visiting museums, but I don't know if I

would want to live in one," he told her. "It seems too cold."

Prue nodded. "I live in my grandmother's old house. It's not filled with major art, but it has a safe, homey feeling."

"Now, that I would like," he told her. "A place that has been around for generations."

She grinned. "You see? We can't forget the past."

He laughed. "Perhaps you are right." He motioned toward a glass display at the far side of the mezzanine. "What did you think of Claiborne's exotic necklace collection?"

"Fabulous, but I couldn't identify two of the pieces," she confessed.

Robert took her hand, and she felt the warmth of his gentle touch swirl through her. He led her across the mezzanine to the glass case. She studied the three necklaces, mentally comparing them to other pieces she'd seen.

"Which one did you identify?" Robert asked.

"The jade and gold one in the middle. It's Chinese—from the Han dynasty, most likely," Prue explained, recognizing the artistry of that period.

"I'm impressed," he said quietly.

She felt the heat rush to her face and peered at Robert, not surprised to find him smiling. "Tell me about the other two," she said.

He pointed to the first necklace. Delicate gold scarabs alternated with gold date-shaped pendants and polished carnelian beads. "The beetles are symbolic of everlasting life," Robert explained. "It is certainly from ancient Egypt. Claiborne swears Cleopatra wore it."

"You sound skeptical," Prue noted.

"That is because it's from the Eighteenth Dynasty, sometime between fifteen and twelve hundred years B.C. Cleopatra reigned between fifty-one and thirty B.C. The dates don't quite line up."

"I see," Prue said, smiling. "And Claiborne doesn't bother with little things like dates?"

"Claiborne knows how old the necklace is. I think he just likes the romance of believing that Cleopatra wore it. And who knows? Perhaps it was passed down to her. Now, this third necklace I have a special affinity for."

He pulled out a small key and unlocked the display case. Then lifted the glass top and slipped his hand beneath the gold chain. Engraved gold surrounded an emerald oval. The gem's smooth surface seemed to pull in the light from the chandelier. Prue couldn't make out the tiny carvings on the gold bezel, but something stirred at the back of her mind. There was something familiar about them.

Robert gingerly lifted the necklace off the velvet display. "I still have a few details to work out with Claiborne, but he's agreed to sell this one to me."

Prue felt a pang of envy shoot through her. She couldn't imagine owning such an exquisite piece of jewelry. "I can't imagine why he'd want to sell it. It's beyond beautiful," she admitted. "It's gorgeous."

"It belongs on someone equally gorgeous," Robert said as he slipped the necklace around her neck.

A mirror framed in gold leaf hung over the display case. Prue glanced at her reflection and the sparkling emerald just below her throat. She watched Robert back away. She turned and met his gaze. "Where are you going?"

"I just want to step back a little so I can see you and the necklace clearly. You belong together."

Prue heard the clock strike midnight. The lights suddenly went out.

"Happy New Year!" everyone yelled at once. Cheers and whistles followed. Prue heard corks popping on champagne bottles and people laughing. Where was Robert?

Fireworks exploded outside in the distance, but they were too far away to illuminate the room. Prue's eyes hadn't adjusted to the darkness yet, but she did realize with startling clarity that she wished Robert hadn't backed away from her.

Okay, she admitted to herself, so I lied about not believing in New Year's Eve traditions, and I really want him to kiss me.

She didn't move, afraid Robert wouldn't be able to find her in the dark. If he just walked straight toward her, she'd be there waiting.

She felt the ruffling of the air in front of her, a light breeze, a gentle movement almost unnoticeable. Then his mouth covered hers. She closed her eyes, feeling as though she were being swept through time.

Her body grew hot. She'd never experienced a kiss this powerful or so completely consuming. She felt as though all her senses had been heightened to focus on and receive Robert's kiss. There was nothing beyond the kiss.

And the kiss—it grew deeper, more intense, until everything melted away except lips against lips, taste, hunger, power.

The lights came back on. The kiss ended. Breathing heavily, Prue slowly opened her eyes as though awakening from a dream. She wanted to lose herself in Robert's blue gaze. She wanted to see in his eyes that he was feeling exactly what she was.

But no one was there.

Turning slightly, she saw Robert standing nearby. Smiling at Prue, he edged around another couple who were kissing. A man bumped into Prue and murmured, "Excuse me," before walking on.

Before Prue could think or react, Robert pulled her close. She wrapped her arms around his neck, wanting to kiss him again. "About time you got back here," she told him.

He lowered his mouth to hers in a sweet romantic kiss.

Desperate to feel what she had before, Prue rose up on her toes, pressing her body against his, expecting him to deepen the kiss. Instead, his mouth moved gently over hers. She didn't feel the excitement, the passion, or the hunger that she had just felt moments earlier.

Robert ended the kiss and smiled warmly. "Better late than never," he said.

Prue stared at him, confused. "What are you talking about?"

"I couldn't find you in the dark," he told her.

Prue felt her heart pounding and the blood thrumming through her temples. "What do you mean?" she asked.

"A kiss at the stroke of midnight would have been so—how do you say—poetic. But a moment later is just as sweet."

Prue gasped as the realization hit her. Robert was not the man she'd kissed at midnight.

But if it wasn't him, who was it?

She jerked her head around, trying to figure out who was the closest, but people were moving quickly, caught up in the celebration. She was grateful that Robert didn't seem to notice her disappointment or confusion.

He held out his hand. "Prue, I need the necklace back so I can return it to Claiborne's display."

"Of course." Prue unlatched the gold chain and handed the necklace to him. She watched him turn to put it back in the case.

"Happy New Year," someone said behind Prue.

She spun around. A tall man stood before her. Prue didn't recognize him, but maybe he was the one who had kissed her so intensely.

She stretched up on her toes, threw her arms around his neck, and kissed him. She needed to know who had made her senses reel. A hunger was opening up inside her that she had to sate.

If she had to, she would kiss every man at the party until she found him, until she discovered the answer to the one question running through her mind.

Who in the world kissed me?

CHAPTER
3

Piper danced to the pulsing music of the Night Owls. She did a quick turn, and Jake spun at the same time. She liked the way he danced. More, she liked the way he kept watching her.

She wished the band would play a slow song, just one slow song—maybe at the stroke of midnight. Jake grabbed her hand and swung her around. She laughed.

The music stopped and with it Piper's obligations returned. Although everything was going smoothly, she was still the manager. She needed to check the kitchen again, make sure the busboys and waiters weren't going crazy, and that the wine and champagne weren't running low. Plus, at some point in the near future, she planned to convince the owner to give everyone who worked on New Year's Eve a bonus.

Breathless, Piper yelled above the din of the crowd, "I've got to go check on Billy to make sure everything is going well in the kitchen."

Jake took her hand. "It's almost midnight. Just one more dance."

Guilt gnawed at Piper. This would be her third or fourth dance. She'd lost track.

Phoebe hurried over as breathless as Piper was. Piper was sure Phoebe had danced nearly every dance.

"Isn't this night amazing?" Phoebe asked Jake.

Jake grinned and looked at Piper. "I'm having a good time. I just wish it wasn't so hard to convince Piper that we need one more dance."

Piper was torn between what she knew she needed to do and what she wanted to do. "Why don't you dance with Phoebe while I check—"

"I'll dance with you both," Jake said as he grabbed Phoebe's and Piper's hands. "Come on. Enjoy the last minutes of the year."

The music started rocking louder and faster than before. Jake was dancing with them both, but he kept looking at Piper. She wished Prue were there to meet this guy. He was so sweet.

She knew when the clock struck midnight that he'd kiss her, and she definitely wanted him to. She hadn't felt this way in a long time.

Someone yelled, "Ten!"

Others joined in, "Nine!"

The countdown had begun. "Eight!"

The music began to slow. "Seven"

Jake released Phoebe's hand. "Six!"

He moved closer to Piper. "Five!"

Bells and whistles sounded. "Four!"

Balloons began falling from the ceiling. "Three."

She wasn't dancing anymore. "Two!"

Jake stared into her eyes. "One!"

"Happy New Year!" everyone screamed.

Jake pulled Piper nearer. "Happy New Year," he said quietly.

She closed her eyes, ready to kiss him, but someone pulled her around. Her eyes opened, and she stared at Billy, his freckled face close to her. "What are you doing?" she asked.

"I had to get your attention. We've got an emergency in the kitchen. One of the pipes under the sink burst, and we've got water all over the floor."

Piper turned away from Billy. "I'm sorry," she told Jake. "I've got to help."

He waved his hand. "Go on. I understand."

Piper followed Billy as he made his way through the crowd. She glanced over her shoulder, looking for Jake through the balloons, streamers, and confetti. Her heart sank when she saw him give Phoebe a small kiss on the cheek.

A kiss that should have been hers.

"This certainly is a very different atmosphere from Claiborne's party," Robert said loudly above the music as he and Prue walked into Quake.

Prue cast him a sideways glance. "I tried to warn you."

"Prue!"

She heard her two sisters shout her name as they rushed to her side. She gave them each a hug. "It looks like the party is a big success."

"It is. And Piper has a new love interest," Phoebe announced.

Piper glared at her sister. "*I'm* not the one he kissed."

"Only because you walked away. Besides, it was a totally innocent kiss. I saw the way he was looking at you. Right now he's back at his table, waiting for you to finish rescuing the kitchen staff. He's not interested in anyone else, Piper."

"It's no fun being responsible on New Year's Eve," Piper grumbled. "We had a little emergency in the kitchen, and it seems I'm the only one who knows how to use a wrench."

Prue grinned at Robert. "The Halliwell women are very practical." She smiled at her sisters as she pulled Robert into the circle. "Robert, these are my sisters, Phoebe and Piper."

"Charmed, ladies," he said as he took Phoebe's hand and kissed it before doing the same with Piper. "Nice to see you again."

"Equally charmed," Phoebe replied.

"Why don't I go to the bar and get us a bottle of champagne so we can toast the New Year." He looked at Prue. "And perhaps new beginnings."

Prue watched him walk away. She liked Robert, but she couldn't stop thinking about the stranger who'd kissed her at midnight. It was crazy to bring Robert to Quake, she told herself. Now he thinks I'm interested.

Phoebe pinched Prue's arm. "So, are you two together now?"

"No. He wanted to come. He caught me at a weak moment, and I thought it would be fun to have him here, but now . . . I'm not so sure."

Prue thought of the romantic kiss Robert had given her at Claiborne's. Maybe that was the problem. Too sweet. She wanted to be kissed passionately, powerfully, like she was at midnight. A strange sensation swept through her, absorbing her, but she couldn't identify what she wanted—what she needed.

"What's wrong?" Phoebe asked.

Prue shook her head. "I just got distracted for a minute, thinking about Claiborne's party."

At Claiborne's she'd been unable to find the man who'd kissed her so intensely. He had disappeared in the crowd—like a phantom—and Prue had tried to find him the only way she knew how. Maybe that was the reason she regretted bringing Robert here. He hadn't seemed too happy watching her kiss other men.

"So what was Claiborne's like?" Phoebe asked.

"It had its moments," Prue answered. She wasn't ready to tell her sisters about the midnight kiss. She wanted to hold on to it, keep it deep inside. But she did have something else to share with them. She grabbed her sisters' hands. "You are not going to believe who crashed the party."

"Brad Pitt?" Piper asked.

Prue rolled her eyes. "Would I have left if he'd been there? No. Elena."

"The tarot reader?" Phoebe asked.

Prue nodded. "It was creepy. She was watching me, and she said she was waiting for her prediction to come true."

"How did she know to go to Claiborne's?" Phoebe asked.

Prue shook her head. "I don't know."

"She was close to our table when she was doing the other reading," Piper admitted. "I guess she could have heard us, or maybe it was just a coincidence."

"So, did her prediction come true? Were you surrounded by an unnatural darkness?" Phoebe asked with a smile.

Prue nodded. "I'd say it was unnatural. I'm wearing red, and everyone, I mean *everyone* else, was wearing black."

Robert returned with four glasses and a bottle of champagne. "Ladies." He handed them each a glass and poured the champagne.

Prue watched the bubbles rise to the surface. She felt as if something was rising inside of her too, some urge she couldn't quite identify.

"To the future," Robert said.

"To the future," the sisters repeated. They all clinked glasses and sipped the champagne.

Just then Prue saw a handsome blond man walking toward them. Her lips tingled. She told herself it was the champagne, but she had the oddest sensation. She wanted to kiss this stranger. Why? she wondered. Her midnight stranger wouldn't be at Quake. It's because he's so good-looking, she told herself.

The blond man stopped beside Piper and smiled at her. "If you're finished with Billy and the kitchen now, I thought maybe we could dance."

Piper's face lit up. "I'd love to." She made quick introductions before handing her glass to Phoebe.

Prue watched Piper walk away with Jake's arm around her. "He's pretty hot," she said. "What was it like when he kissed you, Phoebe?"

Phoebe scoffed. "Short and sweet. It was obvious he's into Piper, not me."

Prue felt heat surge through her as she watched couples dancing and kissing. She wasn't in the mood to dance, but she wanted to get into the spirit of the New Year. She handed her glass to Robert. "Thanks for the champagne."

"Shall we dance?" he asked.

She wrinkled her nose. "I'm not really in the mood."

Prue spotted Billy bursting out of the kitchen with his chef's hat askew. Prue noticed he had a few freckles on his nose. I never realized how cute he is, she thought.

She watched him head toward them, scowling.

"Do you know where Piper is?" Billy asked.

Without thinking, Prue placed her hands on his cheeks and kissed him hard. Pulling back, she grinned broadly, but her smile quickly faded as she looked at Billy.

A gray haze—like a fog—wavered in front of his face. His freckles disappeared. His skin shrank, drawing back slowly, tightening until his face resembled a skull. His eyes grew dull and shadowy.

Prue blinked. The image evaporated like a wisp of smoke that might have never been there. Billy looked fine, his freckles again visible. What kind of champagne had Robert given her to drink?

Billy stared at her, his mouth open. "Gosh, Prue, what was that for?"

Trembling, trying to make sense out of what she'd seen, Prue simply shook her head. She tried to dismiss the whole thing—both the ugly image and the kiss she'd given Billy. "It's the New Year, Billy. Look around. Everyone's kissing. Happy New Year!"

She took his hand. "I'll take you to Piper." She glanced over her shoulder at Robert. "Be right back."

As she led Billy across the restaurant, she felt her lips tingle again. Maybe she should kiss someone else. Prue felt sexy and flirtatious as her eyes roved the crowd. What if her midnight phantom *was* here? she wondered. She fantasized about him following her from Claiborne's party. Even though she didn't know what he looked like, she would never forget him. She thought she might do anything for a man who kissed her the way he had.

Prue shook her head. Get real, she told herself.

He's not here, and kissing men you don't know is not your style.

Still, some part of her couldn't give up hope. Maybe it was the champagne, or maybe it was just the atmosphere of total freedom, of celebrating a new year, when everything was possible. All around her people were giddy, laughing, and kissing as though tomorrow would never come.

For once I want to do something crazy, Prue decided. It's fun to let loose every once in a while. To celebrate!

They reached Piper, and she tapped her sister on the shoulder. "Billy needs you." She looked at Jake. "I'll take Piper's place."

Piper began what seemed like a very long apology to Jake. Prue thought her sister would never leave. Without missing a beat, she moved in to replace Piper as his dance partner. "Phoebe tells me you're a great kisser."

She watched Jake blush. Oh, he is way too cute, Prue thought.

"How could she tell? It was just a quick New Year's kiss," he replied. "On the cheek."

Prue moved in closer, the heat surging through her again. "Let me see if she was right."

She stepped nearer, wrapped her arms around his neck, and moved her lips toward his. He thrust his hand over her mouth, then worked himself free. "Thanks for the offer, Prue, but no thanks."

"It's New Year's," she argued. "What can one little kiss hurt?"

He shook his head. "No offense, but I don't think kissing Piper's sisters before I've kissed her is going get me started on the right foot."

Impatiently Prue waved her hand in the air. "Whatever. I'll find someone else."

She stalked away and saw a couple stop dancing. The woman stepped closer to the man.

Prue remembered how she'd discovered that strong emotions controlled her telekinetic power. And her emotions were very near the surface just then. She was desperate to feel exactly what she'd felt at midnight.

Narrowing her eyes, concentrating on her power, Prue propelled the woman away from her date. She skidded across the room as if hit by a powerful kick. A roar of laughter erupted as the woman stumbled and fell to the ground.

Prue stepped in front of the man. "You don't want her." She wrapped her arms around his neck and pulled his head down for a kiss. But it wasn't any good. It wasn't the one she wanted, the one she was searching for. Surely she could find it again.

She broke off the kiss, stared into the man's face, and watched a foggy haze settle over his features. The man grew pale. Dark gray circles formed around his eyes as they sank back into his sockets.

Prue felt someone shove her aside.

"Get away from him!" the man's girlfriend yelled.

Prue jerked her gaze from the woman to the man. He looked fine again. He grinned brightly.

"Wow! I've never had a kiss like that," he said. The woman punched him in the arm.

"Hey, I'm sorry," he told her, "but it was a great kiss."

Prue looked at the woman and held up her hands in surrender. "I'm sorry. I got carried away. You can have him."

She walked away, her mind swirling. Carried away? she thought. She'd been more than carried away. She knew better than to use her power in public. And the foggy images. Where were they coming from? It made no sense. They were almost like a hallucination.

I feel like I've been drugged, Prue realized. Why am I seeing things that don't exist?

Prue shook her head. She wanted to ignore her craving, but the urge to kiss returned stronger than before. She walked over to a young man with slicked-back hair who was standing alone. Dressed in a neat suit and tie, he looked like a young banker. "Kiss me now," she ordered as she slung her arms around him and pressed her mouth to his.

Dull, dull, dull, she thought a moment later. No passion. No fire. No life. A corpse would probably be a better kisser.

Prue pulled back. The wispy smoke circled the man. She watched his face turn gray. His lips cracked and bled as he gasped for air.

"No! Stop it!" She shoved him away. Feeling dizzy, she pressed her hands to her forehead. Where are these images coming from? Why is my mind playing tricks on me? she wondered. Too much champagne. That has to be it. I just won't drink anymore.

She glanced around the room.

But I've got to have another kiss!

Sitting at the bar with Robert, Phoebe watched Piper dancing with Jake. It hadn't taken Piper long to take care of Billy's problem in the kitchen and get back to the dance floor. Phoebe couldn't blame her. Jake was adorable and a little shy, like Piper. Phoebe thought they made a good pair.

She thought Prue and Robert would make a good pair, too, if Prue would just get back over here. Instead, she seemed intent on kissing every man at Quake. Every man but the one who had walked through the door with her. Phoebe really felt sorry for Robert.

She watched Prue kiss another man, then suddenly push him away. How much has she had to drink? Phoebe wondered. This isn't like Prue at all. It has to be more than the champagne. Is it all an act to make Robert lose interest? she wondered. Still, if Prue doesn't want to get involved in a relationship, the least she could do is be honest with him.

Phoebe turned to Robert, not surprised to see the disappointment in his blue eyes.

"I don't know what's gotten into Prue tonight," Phoebe admitted. "She's not acting like herself at all. I think maybe she's had too much champagne."

Robert held up the glass of champagne Prue had handed him earlier. It was half full. "I don't think that's the problem, Phoebe, but I appreciate your attempt to salvage my pride."

Phoebe propped her elbow on the bar and cradled her chin in her hand. "I've always heard Frenchmen were great kissers."

"Apparently Prue disagrees." He sighed. "I kissed her at Claiborne's. I'd be glad to kiss her again—if she would come near enough."

"How did you meet?"

He shrugged, his gaze shifting back to Prue. "At an auction when I was here last year. We were bidding on the same piece, an Etruscan urn."

"Prue loves bidding wars."

He smiled. "I know. I saw it in her eyes. I could have easily outbid her, but I didn't."

"You let her have it?"

He nodded. "I wanted to get to know her and thought it would be a better gesture than flowers. But she was all business."

"Her career is very important to her," Phoebe told him. She took a quick glance around Quake and saw Prue kiss another guy.

"After I left San Francisco last year, I thought of her every day. So, ever since I returned, I've been trying to get her attention, but she keeps avoiding me. I've tried everything I can think of."

Robert poured Prue's remaining champagne back into the bottle, which struck Phoebe as a little weird. "Things just didn't turn out as I planned," he added bitterly.

He stood, took Phoebe's hand, brought it to his lips, and kissed it gently. "Thank you for keeping me company. Tell Prue if she wants the rest of her champagne to call me."

That was odd, Phoebe thought. Why would he take Prue's champagne with him? She shrugged, watching him walk out of Quake. Phoebe wondered what it would feel like to have such an incredible guy so determined to be with her. She turned her attention back to the dancing couples and the others mingling and talking. She saw Prue wrapped up in kissing another guy who didn't look half as intriguing as Robert.

"Prue, you are nuts," she said quietly.

CHAPTER
4

Prue knew she was dreaming. Yet she'd never had a dream that felt so real. She actually shivered when a light breeze blew over her skin as she stood on the balcony of Lloyd Claiborne's house.

She did not question why she was at Claiborne's. It was here, in this house, that she had experienced the unbelievable kiss, and she wanted to experience it again.

Prue watched dawn ease over the horizon, the sunlight slowly making its way across the water, sparkling as it touched waves created by the breeze. Such a beautiful way to begin New Year's Day, she thought, and headed inside from the balcony.

She descended the marble staircase to the mezzanine overlooking the first floor. In the misty world between sleep and waking, she might discover the man behind the kiss in the very spot where he had first kissed her.

She felt someone touch her waist lightly. Her heart sped up and her lips tingled. She knew without looking that it was him, the one who had stirred the fires of passion within her. Now she would learn who he was. She would see his face, his eyes, his smile. She would know all there was to know about him. She began to turn.

"No," he whispered. "Don't turn around yet."

He lifted her black hair and his lips touched the side of her neck. Warm shivers cascaded through her body.

"Of all the things I have seen, things from centuries past, you are the most beautiful," he said in a low voice. "I feel as though I've waited all my life to meet you, to know you, to have you."

He trailed his mouth up and down the nape of her neck. "Your kiss gives me life," he said.

And *his* kisses went through her like wildfire.

Prue turned to look at him. Shadows cast by the hooded robe he wore concealed his face. She wanted to reach up and push the hood away, but she somehow knew that if she did, the dream would fade and so would he.

"Do you recognize me?" he asked.

"Only by the feel of your kiss," she answered.

"That is how it should be." He cupped her face with his palms and brought her into the shadows with him. He lowered his mouth to hers, and she felt the hunger rush through her. She wrapped her arms around him, pressing her body against his.

His lips were like twin flames, burning with passion, filling her with a need, a desire, to kiss him for eternity.

He said her kiss gave him life. He needed her. He wanted her.

Everything else in her life lost all significance.

Much later that morning, Phoebe sat at the kitchen table, doodling on a pad of paper and trying to make some kind of plan for the New Year. But her mind kept drifting back to Prue's odd behavior the night before.

Maybe Prue just got caught up in the spirit of the evening, she thought. After all, a lot of people were letting loose. Phoebe shook her head. But I still feel sorry for Robert.

She glanced up at the echo of footsteps on the stairs.

Piper shuffled into the room and dropped into a chair with a moan. "Oh, my aching feet. I never danced that much in my whole life."

"I wonder how Prue's feeling this morning. She doesn't usually sleep this late," Phoebe said.

Piper leaned forward, her brows furrowed. "What got into her last night? I saw her kissing guys she couldn't possibly have known."

"I thought it was strange too, not to mention rude. She told Robert she'd be right back, so he waited, but Prue was too busy kissing every male in sight. Finally Robert left."

"Well, she'll probably regret last night in more ways than one," Piper replied. "Prue's going to have one heavy-duty hangover when she gets up." She reached for the box of doughnuts sitting on the table. "I see we're having a nutritious breakfast this morning."

"I thought we should start the New Year off right," Phoebe said with a laugh, wondering how things had ended with Piper and Jake the night before. "Jake is pretty cute. Any plans to see him again?"

Piper smiled. "As a matter of fact, we're going out later this week."

"That's great!" Phoebe cried. Piper had shied away from guys after the Jeremy disaster. Not that Phoebe blamed her, but she was glad to see Piper was willing to give Jake a chance. Phoebe had a good feeling about the two of them.

"It'll be great as long he doesn't turn out to be a warlock," Piper said. Her voice was teasing, but Phoebe caught the undercurrent of fear.

"It's going to be all right, Piper," Phoebe assured her, hoping madly that she was right. Piper had had one horrible experience. She didn't need another one.

"I don't suppose you had a premonition when he kissed you on the cheek last night?" Piper asked.

Phoebe squinted. "I did see you in a white dress . . . and he was at a church."

Piper lightly brushed her hand over Phoebe's arm. "You're making that up."

Phoebe smiled. "Yeah, I am. Sorry, no visions. Not yet anyway."

Piper grabbed the pad Phoebe had been drawing on. "What's this?"

"I was just playing," Phoebe said, a little embarrassed at being caught. She liked to draw, had even considered art school for a while, but then she got sidetracked. Phoebe couldn't even remember by what.

Piper's eyes widened. "You call this playing? It's fantastic, Phoebe. I had no idea you were so artistic."

"It helps me focus when I'm trying to work things out," Phoebe said.

"Well, Quake needs new stationery," Piper said. "I've been looking for an artist I could afford and haven't had any luck. Do you want to design it?"

Thrilled with the offer, Phoebe grinned and squeezed Piper's arm. "I'd love to. Hey, maybe Elena was right, and money will come my way."

"I was hoping you'd do it as a favor." Piper smiled weakly. "You know, one sister for another."

"Maybe we can work out a trade." Phoebe felt the excitement mounting at the prospect of actually doing something useful for a change. "You can do my laundry for a week. Besides, it's a beginning. I'll have something to put in my portfolio if I ever decide to get serious about being an artist."

"You know, Phoebe, you really need to decide what you want to do with your life," Piper said.

"Does anyone really know what they want to

do with their life?" Prue asked as she walked into the kitchen and poured herself a cup of coffee.

Phoebe and Piper exchanged glances. "Yesterday you did," Phoebe reminded her. "You wanted to concentrate on your career."

Sitting at the table, Prue smiled. "That was yesterday."

"So, what are you concentrating on today? Or should I say *who?*" Phoebe asked.

"Yeah," Piper added. "You said you didn't want to get involved with Robert, then you bring him to Quake, then you ignore him. What's up with that?"

Prue lifted a shoulder and stared into her coffee. "Robert's really nice, but . . ."

"But what?" Phoebe pressed her.

Prue took a sip of her coffee before looking at her sisters. "Last night at Claiborne's party, the lights went out at midnight. A man kissed me. It was the most incredible kiss of my life."

Phoebe shot a glance at Piper. She looked as confused as Phoebe felt. Why hadn't Prue mentioned this last night?

"A man?" Phoebe asked. "What man?"

"That's the problem," Prue said. "I don't know who he is. When the lights came back on, I opened my eyes and he was gone." She smiled. "I've been thinking of him as the midnight phantom."

Piper laughed. "Very comic book." Then she looked at Prue more carefully. "You're not serious, are you?"

Prue held up a hand. "I know it sounds silly, but I don't know what else to call him."

"Wait a minute," Phoebe said. "This doesn't add up. You brought Robert to Quake—from Claiborne's party. Robert even told me he kissed you at Claiborne's. So, why isn't the midnight phantom Robert, who happens to be gorgeous and charming, et cetera?"

Prue shook her head. "He wasn't the one who kissed me at midnight. At first I thought it was him. We were talking, but he moved away just before the lights went out. When they came back on, there were all these people between us. I don't think it was him."

"Still, he *did* kiss you," Phoebe pointed out, refusing to give up on Robert.

Prue nodded. "A little later, but it was definitely not the same kiss. Robert's was sweet and gentle. The kiss at midnight was . . . powerful. I can't describe it. It was as if it absorbed every part of me."

Phoebe stared at her sister, trying to make sense of what had happened. "But when the lights came on, this guy must have been standing in front of you, right?"

"No, no one was there when the lights came back on. I guess he moved away quickly."

"Like he was shy?" Piper asked.

"Believe me," Prue assured her. "He wasn't shy."

"Then why did he move away?" Phoebe asked, more confused than ever.

A dreamy expression crossed Prue's face. "I don't know. I tried to find him. I want to know who he is. This morning I dreamed that he was kissing me at Claiborne's mansion. I couldn't see his face, but his kiss was so incredible. The dream was so real. I felt as though I'd stepped into another world."

"No wonder you slept so late," Piper said. "Sounds like a dream you wouldn't want to wake up from."

Prue gave a sigh of resignation. "But I did wake up . . . so I might as well make the best of it." She stared out the window for a moment, then turned to her sisters. "I know. We didn't get to see that much of one another last night. It's a really nice day out. So why don't we go on a picnic today at Golden Gate Park?"

"Sounds good," Phoebe said. She loved picnics and being outdoors. Still, something about the night before bothered her. "Of course, you would have seen more of us if you hadn't been so busy kissing every guy at Quake," she added.

"I didn't kiss every guy," Prue assured her in a casual tone. "Just the cute ones."

Phoebe watched a surprised look cross Piper's face, and she was sure that she and Piper were having the identical thought: Is this *our* Prue talking?

That afternoon Piper stared out the kitchen window at the clear blue sky. It was a warm, balmy day for January, a wonderful way to begin the New Year. She was glad Prue had suggested the picnic in Golden Gate Park.

She heard Prue and Phoebe talking behind her as they made sandwiches, but she wasn't interested in the conversation. Absently she stirred the lemonade they were going to take with them, her thoughts drifting to Jake.

She really liked talking with him and dancing with him and just plain looking at him. If only Billy hadn't stopped her from kissing Jake, the night would have been perfect.

Still, Jake had invited her to the premiere of a movie that had been filmed in San Francisco. It turned out he even had a totally cool job. He was a set designer and had worked on the film.

She thought about the purple silk gown she'd just ordered from a catalogue for the premiere. It looked like the kind all the stars wore to Hollywood premieres. Would it work in San Francisco? It would have to, Piper told herself.

The shrill ring of the phone drew her out of her thoughts. She grabbed the receiver. "Hello?"

"Happy New Year, Piper," Robert said. "How are you?"

"I'm fine." Smiling, she leaned against the counter, wiggled her brows at Prue, pointed to the phone, and mouthed, "Robert."

"Is Prue there?" he asked.

Prue shook her head vehemently and waved her hands back and forth. She didn't understand Prue's reaction, but sisterly loyalty made her say, "I'm sorry, Robert, she's not here."

"Will you tell her I called?"

"Sure. I'll tell her," Piper said. "Happy New Year." She hung up and saw Phoebe glaring at Prue.

"What is your problem?" Phoebe asked. "I talked with him for an hour last night. He's nice and considerate, funny and smart."

"I'm just not into him." Prue shrugged. "I should probably take a shower before we go to the park."

Piper and Phoebe exchanged a baffled glance. Sometimes their extremely sensible sister made no sense at all.

The phone rang again. Piper snatched up the receiver. "Hello?"

"Hello, this is Claire from Buckland's. You have to put Prue on the phone. Is she there? Is she all right? I need to talk to her. Put her on—quick!"

Piper heard the hysterical edge in the woman's voice. "Just a minute, Claire. I'll get her."

She handed the phone to Prue and stepped back, watching as Prue rolled her eyes. "Relax, Claire, I'm fine."

"Why are you looking so worried?" Phoebe whispered as she came to stand beside Piper.

"It's Prue's boss," Piper said, glancing at Prue. "She's kind of having a nervous breakdown."

"I'll be there, Claire. Don't worry," Piper heard Prue say.

Piper watched Prue hang up the phone. "What was all that about?" she asked. "Claire sounded freaked."

"There's a big client coming in, and I'm supposed to run the meeting," Prue said. "Claire wanted to make sure I'd be at work tomorrow."

"Why wouldn't you be?" Piper asked.

"Some people at Claiborne's party suddenly got sick," Prue told her. "And whatever they've got, it hit fast and hard. They're all in the hospital."

Prue watched Piper toss the Frisbee to Phoebe. They'd had a wonderful, lazy picnic. Good food, perfect weather, and lots of time to talk about stuff they all thought they'd forgotten—their junior-high history teacher who was dyslexic with numbers and had them all convinced that the Civil War took place in the 1680s; Phoebe's cutting school when she was twelve to get a rock star's autograph, only to find out his concert was canceled; Piper's teddy bear that somehow wound up winning a free subscription to a magazine.

"And for years," Piper said as she bent to retrieve the Frisbee, "I got golf magazines addressed to Mr. Ted Halliwell."

"That's right," Phoebe added. "Didn't someone send him a little box of tees and some free golf shoes? I was sure he was going to enter a tournament."

Prue smiled, enjoying the memories. We need to spend more time together, she decided. That will be my New Year's resolution: to spend more time with my sisters.

The Frisbee came sailing toward her, then arced up and floated high overhead.

Prue jumped to catch the Frisbee, but her fingers barely skimmed it. She landed on the ground and planted her hands on her hips. "Who do you think I am, Piper? Michael Jordan?"

"Hurry up and get it, Prue," Phoebe yelled to her.

Prue rolled her eyes and raced after the Frisbee. She spotted it near a walkway where some college guys were skateboarding. She skidded to a stop and watched, fascinated by their skills. One guy was especially good. He sailed into a jump, spun around, and landed perfectly, defying gravity and half the laws of physics.

Skateboarding had never really appealed to Prue, but this guy did. Holding her gaze, he smiled broadly and performed a series of daring turns, jumps, and flips.

A small thrill shot through her when she realized he was showing off for her. Usually that kind of display turned her off completely, but not this time. This time she watched, mesmerized. She felt heat begin to emerge throughout her body, felt her lips tingle. Desire threaded through her.

The guy ended his performance. Prue clapped. He stomped on his skateboard with one foot, and it flew into his hand. He sauntered over to her.

"Hey, how's it going?" he asked casually.

"You tell me," she said in a low, throaty voice as she braced her palms on either side of his face and pressed her mouth against his in a passionate kiss.

She was so caught up in the kiss that she barely heard Phoebe's outraged "Prue!"

Calm down, Phoebe, she thought. He's harmless. She pulled away from the skateboarder—and gasped when she caught sight of his face. A smoky mirage formed before her eyes, just as it had with the men she kissed the night before!

Prue cringed as the skateboarder's skin began to shrivel and grow taut over his cheekbones. His cheeks caved in until she saw the outline of his jaw. His lips pulled back to reveal receding gums. He moaned as his blackened tongue rolled out of his mouth.

Closing her eyes, Prue stepped back. What's happening? she wondered. Why am I seeing these things?

She opened her eyes, relieved to see the skateboarder grinning again, looking perfectly healthy, totally adorable. She leaned in for another kiss.

This time she heard both Phoebe and Piper yell, "Prue!"

What is their problem? she thought with resentment.

She leaned away from the guy. The fog was back in place. His pale, emaciated face was worse than before. His lips were blackened and blistered. The stench of his rotting flesh assailed her nostrils. His desiccated skin and muscle fell from his forehead, his cheeks, his nose in bleeding chunks, piece after piece, revealing bones. Bones that began to crumble and blow in the wind like bits of sand on the desert.

Gasping for breath, she backed away. A horrifying realization hit her.

I've just kissed Death!

CHAPTER
5

W**hy are you** staring at me like that?" the skateboarder asked Prue.

Repulsed, Prue closed her eyes and shook her head. "I-I'm sorry," she managed to say.

"I'm not," he said. "Can I have your phone number?"

She opened her eyes. He looks perfectly normal, she realized as a shiver crawled up her spine. What is going on?

She shook her head. "I—I don't give out my phone number."

He frowned, looking a little confused. "Well, if you change your mind, you can usually find me around here." His skateboard hit the walkway with a resounding crash. He jumped onto it and took off.

Prue breathed a sigh of relief as he joined his

friends. She watched them laugh and slap him on the back as though he'd accomplished a minor miracle. He was way younger than she was, and she'd kissed him with wild abandon.

Why does that horrible image emerge every time I kiss someone? Prue wondered. When did this all start happening? Prue couldn't be sure.

Quake, she realized. It definitely happened at Quake. I thought it was from all the champagne, but I haven't had anything at all to drink today.

She shuddered, unable to shake off the ominous feeling of dread whirling through her. Something was wrong. She rubbed her forehead, suddenly feeling very tired. Maybe I'm coming down with the flu or something.

Reaching down, she grabbed the Frisbee from the grass and slowly walked back to her sisters.

"What were you doing?" Phoebe asked. "How could you kiss a total stranger?"

"He didn't seem to mind. Besides, who I kiss is none of your business. I—" Prue broke off, appalled. Where had the harshness in her voice come from?

Prue tried to gather her thoughts, finding the task difficult. Her mind didn't seem to want to cooperate. What's happening? she wondered. I can't seem to concentrate. I keep thinking about that midnight kiss and wanting to find it again.

"Prue, are you okay?" Phoebe sounded worried.

"I can't explain it. I see a cute guy, and I get this incredible urge to kiss him," Prue said, unable to describe exactly what was going on inside her. It was more than an urge. It was becoming an obsession.

"New Year's, I can understand," Phoebe said. "Everyone was kissing everyone. People were caught up in the moment. But that guy on the skateboard—"

"Haven't you ever done something you regretted?" Prue asked, trying to explain to her sisters what she herself didn't understand. The frightening visions of these guys turning into corpses . . .

"We've all done something we regretted," Piper told her.

Phoebe laughed. "Like the time I went out with that guy who insisted on wearing leather in the summertime?"

"Yeah." Piper laughed too. She pinched her nose with her fingers. "P.U."

Frustrated by her sisters' laughter, Prue felt her body tense. The last thing she needed or wanted was laughter. What she wanted was another kiss. It was all she thought about. The intensity of her obsession scared her.

She looked intently at both her sisters. "This is going to sound incredibly strange," she said, "but it's like I'm . . . addicted to kissing."

"Prue, people get addicted to drugs or alcohol," Piper pointed out. "Not kisses."

"Don't you think I know that?" Prue asked, her mind whirling. No matter what she tried to concentrate on, her thoughts kept returning to one: Kiss someone else. Find someone else to kiss.

"Prue, you didn't look as if you enjoyed kissing that skateboarder," Phoebe said.

"It's not that," Prue said. She touched Phoebe's arm. "It's when I *stop* kissing that I regret it. Then I wish I hadn't done it in the first place."

"Then why do it if you know you're going to regret it later?" Phoebe asked.

"I don't know! I just know I have to!" Prue shouted. "And I will kiss *whomever* I want, *whenever* I want!"

Shocked by her words, Prue stepped back. Her sisters were staring at her as though she'd lost her mind.

"Prue, what's wrong with you?" Piper asked.

"Nothing's wrong with me," Prue snapped. "You just don't understand." She tossed them the Frisbee and began to walk off. She'd had enough of her sisters and trying to explain to them what she was feeling. It was none of their business anyway.

But it is their business, she argued with herself. I want them to understand, to help me figure out what is happening. I need to tell them about the visions. I will tell them about the visions—later.

First I need another kiss.

Two days later Piper hung up the phone, her hands shaking. She stared out the window, only half listening to Prue and Phoebe as they talked over breakfast.

Oh, those poor people, she thought. Please let them get better. Please, please, let them get well.

"Hey, Piper, what's wrong?" Prue asked. "Who was on the phone? You look like someone died."

Unbelievable fear and guilt wove through Piper as she faced her sisters. Is this my fault? she wondered.

"That was the owner of Quake," she explained. "Several people who were at the party on New Year's Eve are in the hospital. They're really sick. The Board of Health is investigating the restaurant."

"Why is the Board of Health investigating?" Phoebe asked, clearly stunned.

Worried, Piper stared at the floor, trying to absorb the full impact of what the owner had told her. I might get fired, she realized. Maybe I deserve to get fired.

"It's their job," she explained in a bleak voice. "Even though the people in the hospital don't show any typical symptoms of food poisoning. They don't have upset stomachs or fevers. . . ." She shook her head vehemently. "I don't understand how this happened. It can't be food poisoning. We use fresh ingredients, and I make sure the employees wash their hands before they touch food or serve it."

Phoebe hurried to Piper and hugged her. "It's not your fault," she reassured her. "Sometimes restaurants get tainted food."

But Piper still felt that she was to blame. She was the manager. And that wasn't the worst of it. The sick people weren't all strangers. "Billy's sick, too."

"Your assistant chef?" Prue asked.

Piper nodded, her chest aching. Billy constantly sampled the food he prepared. Maybe they'd gotten some bad beef or seafood. "He's in the hospital."

Prue rose from the table, crossed the kitchen, and put her arm around Piper's shoulders. "Don't worry. You can't do anything about it. Those people in the hospital—they all will get well."

"And besides, tonight is the big night." Phoebe smiled softly. "Your first date with Jake."

"And he's taking you to a premiere! I don't suppose you'd consider slipping me into your purse? I hear it's a great movie," Prue teased.

Piper forced herself to laugh when she really wanted to cry, thinking about all those sick people. "I thought you said we couldn't do shrinking spells."

Prue rubbed Piper's cheek. "I did, but at least it made you smile."

Piper heard the doorbell ring. "I'll get it," she said. "Maybe it's my dress for tonight."

She opened the door to a scrawny man with greasy red hair and thick glasses dressed in a gray uniform. He gave her a goofy smile. He reminded her of an overanxious puppy wanting attention.

"I've got a package here for Piper Halliwell," he announced in a deep voice that she suspected was put on to make him sound more masculine.

"That would be me," she said as she took the package from him and glanced at the return address. It *was* the dress! She wanted to look spectacular when she went out with Jake. Irresistible would work too.

"I need you to sign right here," the delivery guy said, extending a clipboard toward her.

Piper set the package aside before taking the clipboard and pen. She began to sign her name.

"Hi there, handsome."

She glanced up with surprise at the sound of Prue's voice and her words. Handsome? she thought. Since when did *nerd* translate into *handsome?*

Bewildered, she watched Prue grab the guy and plant her lips squarely on his. Is Prue totally out of her mind? she wondered, unable to believe what she was seeing.

Piper stared at her sister and the guy's flailing arms. He broke away, looking alarmed and bewildered. He grabbed the clipboard from Piper and raced to his van.

Piper watched Prue slump against the door, her eyes closed, a deep furrow in her brow.

"Have you gone totally nuts?" Piper asked. "You can't honestly tell me you thought that guy was good-looking."

Prue opened her eyes. Piper saw the confusion on her sister's face as she shook her head. "No, he wasn't."

"Then why did you kiss him?" Piper demanded.

Prue shrugged, her voice filled with doubt. "I—I don't know." Suddenly she straightened, shook her head, and smiled. "I guess I just needed a kiss, and he was available." She wiggled her fingers. "See you. I'm off to work."

Piper watched her sister walk casually to her car, get in, and drive off. What is going on? Piper wondered. It was like I was talking to two different Prues.

"Tell me I did not see her kiss that funny-looking delivery guy," Phoebe said.

"I wish I could," Piper replied, still stunned by the scene. "It was so strange. You should have seen her face after she kissed him. She looked as if she really didn't want to do it, as if she forced herself."

"Something is definitely wrong," Phoebe said. "That is not the Prue we know and love."

"No kidding. I'm worried about her," Piper admitted. "I feel like I'm talking to a stranger."

Piper glanced at her watch and grimaced. "Whoa, I've got to get to Quake to see what the Board of Health has to say. I'm sure I'll have to answer a million questions." She squeezed Phoebe's hand. "Let's try to figure out what's wrong with Prue, okay?"

"Maybe she's having a midlife crisis," Phoebe suggested.

"At twenty-seven? I don't think so." Piper headed for her car, an ominous sense of foreboding shadowing her as she thought about the expression on Prue's face before and after she kissed the guy. Revulsion, she thought. Prue didn't want to kiss that guy. She didn't enjoy it. So why is she doing it?

No matter how she looked at it, Piper couldn't shake the feeling that something was terribly wrong with Prue.

Phoebe walked through the empty house, unable to stop thinking about Prue's strange behavior.

New Year's Eve she wrote off to the atmosphere at Quake. But the guy on the skateboard? And the super-nerd delivery man?

She cleared off the kitchen table, put the dirty dishes into the dishwasher, and began to wipe down the counter. Idly she lifted up a written phone message and was about to put it back, when a word caught her eye. "Robert."

She looked at the note more closely: "Prue, Robert called to say he has tickets to a play for Friday night. He wants to know if you'd be interested in going with him. My advice, whether you want it or not, is a big fat YES! He'll call you again. Piper."

Phoebe ran her fingers over the words. Robert. Prue had brought him to Quake and then left him while she kissed every guy in sight.

Robert told me he'd done all he could to get Prue's attention, she remembered. *All he could.*

What did that mean? she wondered. In a normal world, maybe flowers, poetry, soft music, and candles. But in *our* world . . . she couldn't help but think of spells, potions, and incantations.

Why did Robert take Prue's champagne with him? Had he somehow managed to slip something into her drink? A love potion that had back-fired?

Phoebe's heart thundered as she considered the possibility that Robert might be of their world. She tried to convince herself that she was getting carried away, that Robert was just a regular guy. But she kept picturing Robert as he poured Prue's champagne back into the bottle, and the unsettling feeling she suddenly had about him wouldn't leave.

She rushed through the kitchen and up the stairs to the attic. She threw open the door and walked to the podium in the center of the room where they kept *The Book of Shadows*.

She placed her hands on the thick leather-bound book and closed her eyes, hoping for a vision, a sign of where to look inside the book for the answers, but nothing came to her.

"Fine, then," she mumbled as she opened the book and began thumbing through the pages. Robert can't be of our world, she thought. I don't want him to be.

"Something must have happened to Prue New Year's Eve," Phoebe muttered to herself. "Something that would explain why she is now so obsessed with kissing guys. But what?"

The problem with magic was that it was so complex. There were countless spells and charms that another witch or a warlock could use. And then there were mistakes. One wrong word, one incorrect ingredient, and a spell for good could become a spell for evil.

Phoebe stopped turning pages when the words "kisses sweet" caught her eye. Prue said Robert's kiss was sweet, Phoebe remembered. It wasn't filled with passion like the kiss she received at midnight.

Slowly Phoebe read the spell:

> For kisses sweet to turn to passion,
> You must be willing to take this action.
> With a potion sweeter than wine,
> Make the one you love become thine.
> But beware, for if you falter,
> You lose your chance,
> And this spell you can never alter.

"A love spell that involves a potion," Phoebe whispered as a shiver went through her.

Robert said that he had done everything he could to get Prue's attention, and things had not turned out the way he had planned. And then he took Prue's champagne with him.

Were you going to drink it yourself, Robert, so it wasn't wasted? Or did it contain something that you didn't want anyone else to drink?

This whole idea made Phoebe feel queasy. She closed *The Book of Shadows* and laid her head on it. A feeling of dread was creeping into her. Maybe Robert wasn't the great guy she took him for. If he used this spell, then he knows magic, she conceded.

An even worse thought flashed through her mind. And if he's using magic *against* Prue, then he's probably a warlock!

CHAPTER
6

Although dressed in her dark purple gown and holding Jake's hand, Piper was having a hard time dealing with where she was.

The hospital. Where Billy was fighting for his life.

She'd wanted to visit Billy earlier, but the Board of Health kept her tied up all day. So when Jake picked her up for their date, she asked if they could stop by the hospital first.

Now she glanced over at Jake, walking beside her in his black tuxedo. He took her breath away. Besides being totally gorgeous, he is one of the nicest guys I've ever met, she thought, and she squeezed his hand. "Thanks for agreeing to this little detour."

"No problem," Jake said with a smile.

But his smile was a little stiff, and there was something in his voice that didn't ring true.

"Somehow I'm getting the idea that there is a problem," Piper said warily.

"I'm just trying to understand your relationship with Billy. I could tell on New Year's Eve that he's important to you. I guess I'm wondering how important," Jake admitted.

Piper felt the warmth creep into her face, slightly embarrassed now that she'd unknowingly taken some of the excitement for the date away from him. "Are you jealous?" she asked.

He shrugged. "Yeah, I guess I am. Which makes me feel like a jerk, since the guy is sick."

"Billy and I are just friends," she explained.

He glanced down at the floor. "So I'm a total jerk."

"I think you're sweet," she said. He met her gaze, and she smiled. "You must like me if you're jealous."

His eyes held hers. "I like you a lot, Piper."

"We won't stay long," she promised as they arrived at Billy's room.

Holding Jake's hand, she tiptoed inside. A curtain was draped around Billy's bed. She moved it aside, and her heart constricted at the sight of her assistant chef. He looked as though he'd lost half his body weight. Shadows circled his eyes, and his skin had a grayish tint to it.

She took his hand. It felt cool and clammy, and she knew that wasn't a good sign. "Oh, Billy," she murmured.

He opened his eyes and gave her a weak smile. "You probably shouldn't hold my hand, Piper.

They don't know what's wrong with me. It might be contagious."

"If they thought it was contagious, they wouldn't have let me in." She brushed the hair off his sweat-beaded brow. "Are you in pain?"

He shook his head. "Just tired. Thanks for the flowers. I wish I could smell them."

She glanced quickly at the arrangement of roses sitting on the table beside his bed. "I guess sending flowers to a guy is kind of dumb. Tomorrow I'll bring you something good to eat."

"You look pretty," Billy said quietly.

She pointed at Jake, who stood behind her. "Jake got us tickets to the opening of *A Summer Night's Longing*. It was shot downtown."

"I remember," Billy said with a sigh.

He seemed to be weakening as she stood there, watching, and his eyes became more sunken.

"Piper, I'm sorry, but we're going to have to go," Jake said in a low voice beside her.

She nodded. "I know." She squeezed Billy's hand. "I'll see you tomorrow."

He barely nodded, closed his eyes, and drifted off to sleep.

"I feel responsible," Piper told Jake as they left the room.

"You didn't do anything to make him or anyone else get sick." He placed an arm around her shoulders. "Piper, I was at Quake. I ate the food, drank the champagne. Do I look like I'm on the verge of checking myself into the hospital?"

She studied him closely—his tanned skin, his

eyes shining at her, his strong voice. "No, as a matter of fact, you look exceptionally fine." Piper's heart still ached for Billy, but she forced herself to smile. "I've been looking forward to this evening all week."

He grinned. "Really?"

"Are you kidding? It's my first premiere."

She gazed at him, liking the shape of his mouth, the warmth in his eyes, the curve of his lips, the line of his nose—everything about him.

Outside the hospital a white limousine waited for them. Piper felt a thrill of excitement go through her as the chauffeur opened the door, and she and Jake climbed into the backseat.

"I'm not used to this kind of luxury," she admitted as the limousine pulled away from the hospital.

"The glamorous life has its ups and downs," he told her with a grin.

"Tell me about the down part," Piper said, curious.

"First of all, I don't always ride around in limos. This is just for the premiere—I figured we had to arrive in style. The day-to-day stuff isn't all that dazzling. I spend a lot of time staring at my drawing board or my computer screen. And the hours can get long. Half the time, a director describes how he wants the set to look, then you design and build it, and he tells you that it's not at all what he had in mind."

"But you like your work?"

"Love it," he admitted. "It makes me view things differently."

"What do you mean?"

Jake squinted and placed his hand to his eye as if looking through a lens. "I tend to look at every space as a set, as a place where a certain kind of scene can come alive," he explained. "For example, I bet what you see right now is the two of us riding in a limo."

Piper blinked and looked around her. "That's because we are riding in a limo."

He shifted so that he faced her. "Sometimes a set can be as small as the inside of a car. Let's say the story has a scene, and the hero is taking the heroine to a movie premiere, and he's trying to decide whether she'll let him kiss her before they get to the movie." He pushed a button on the panel beside him, and soft music floated into the car. "Should the set—the interior of the car—have that button so he can play music for her?"

Piper smiled and slowly touched her hand to his arm, thinking it'd be very nice if he'd put that arm around her again. "The set should definitely have that button," she answered.

Jake placed his arm around her and drew her close. Piper's heart raced as he trailed his finger along her cheek.

"Should the set have lights or muted shadows?" he asked.

"Muted shadows," she whispered, getting lost in the brown of his eyes.

"Well, then there's a risk. A set like this might make the hero kiss the heroine before he should."

"No risk," Piper murmured. "The feeling is definitely mutual."

"Really?" he asked as he brought her closer to him.

Yes, her mind screamed. Kiss me. Kiss me now.

The limousine stopped in front of the theater. Jake groaned. "Maybe the hero should talk faster."

Piper laughed at the disappointment on his face, feeling exactly the same way. She'd been primed for a little more intimacy. When the evening ends, she thought. "At least you've set the stage for the drive home."

He smiled. "I hope so."

He took her hand. "Come on, and don't be nervous. There will be a crowd of cheering people and cameras going off like crazy until everyone realizes we're not movie stars."

Piper took a deep breath, her nerves suddenly on edge as she looked out the window. Jake was right. The place was packed with fans standing behind ropes and barriers. The chauffeur opened the door and Jake got out first. Then he helped Piper out.

Lightbulbs flashed and TV cameras rolled. With her arm wrapped around Jake's, Piper felt like a star, someone exciting and important. Walking along the red carpet, she knew she would remember this night for as long as she lived.

The crowd closed in as several of the real stars arrived. Suddenly Piper was surrounded by reporters. She clung to Jake's arm, trying not to lose him as he forged a way through the throng.

Jake quickened his pace and Piper felt a tug on her gown. She glanced back. A tall woman in spike heels had unknowingly stepped firmly on the hem of Piper's long, flowing skirt. Piper couldn't pull it free.

Jake tugged on Piper's arm—and she heard a soft ripping sound. She tried to stop him. "Jake!"

But he didn't hear her over the noise of the crowd and kept walking.

Another ragged sound of fabric being torn apart brought Piper to a halt. She suddenly felt the chill night air swirl around her legs. She glanced down and let out a cry.

Her skirt was gone!

Mortified, Piper flung out her hands and froze time. The front of the theater became silent. Cameras stopped flashing, people stood with mouths agape, eyes wide, hands reaching out.

Piper glared at the pool of purple silk on the ground—all that remained of the skirt of her beautiful gown. Bending down, she worked the cloth free from under the woman's shoe, snatched it up, and looked at Jake. His eyes were closed against the blinding flash of a camera.

I've got to get out of here before time unfreezes, she realized.

With regret she placed her hand on Jake's

cheek. "I'm sorry, Jake," she whispered. "I won't be here for the ride home."

She wrapped her skirt around her waist and tied it in place. Then, with her legs pumping and her heart pounding, she started running, disappearing into a long line of fans that stretched down the street.

Seconds later she heard the sounds of the crowd again. Time was no longer frozen. Piper glanced over her shoulder. She caught a glimpse of Jake, a bewildered look on his face as he spun around, obviously looking for her.

"Piper!" he yelled.

She wanted to call out to him, to go to him, but she couldn't. Not like this, with half her dress torn off.

As quickly as she could, she wove her way through the crowd—a magical night ending with a disappearing act.

Sitting at her desk at Buckland's, Prue swiveled around to glance out the window. Dusk was settling over the city, which meant that Piper should be at the movie premiere with Jake now.

The glamour of Hollywood in the Bay Area, Prue thought. It wasn't exactly Piper's style, but Prue knew her sister would find a way to fit in. She hoped Piper was having fun; she really needed some after the whole health department scandal.

Prue rubbed her eyes and turned back to the thick reference books on her desk. She couldn't remember ever feeling quite this drained after a day at the auction house.

Usually, her work gave her energy—especially when she was doing the kind of research that she was working on now. She loved uncovering the history of a piece of art, imagining whose hands it had passed through, the places where it might have been.

She found a description of the type of vase she was cataloguing, and stared at the page until the words became illegible and the room began to fade into shadows.

She considered going home, but she'd didn't like driving when she was so tired.

I'll just close my eyes for a minute, she told herself. A quick nap and I'll feel better.

She felt herself drifting off into that world between waking and sleeping, the place where her dreams took on the guise of reality.

And then she felt his presence. It was the man who kissed her—the midnight phantom.

He's here, she realized. In this room with me, surrounding me. And it's real. I can hear my heart pounding, feel my blood pulsing.

He stepped closer, his form visible but his face still shrouded in shadows.

She fought a surge of disappointment. She wanted to see his face. And then she knew that it didn't really matter. We have a connection, she realized, a bond that nothing can break.

"You give me life," she heard him whisper just before his mouth covered hers.

She felt as though he were a magnet, that his power drew her to him in a way she couldn't begin to resist. Not that she wanted to resist. She could feel a current of energy dancing between them, giving and draining, giving and draining.

Her heart pounded, her temples throbbed. Her body burned with longing. She wanted the kiss to last into eternity.

He drew away, leaving her breathless, gasping for breath, and desperate for another touch of his lips.

Within the dream she opened her eyes. She saw his hands spread apart as they held a necklace with a large hanging emerald. She blinked. It was the necklace Robert had shown her at Claiborne's—the one he was going to auction. How had this stranger gotten it? Why does he have it?

He placed it around her neck, and the emerald came to rest just below her throat.

"This is my gift to you," he whispered. "To wear in life, and then in death."

Prue snapped out of the dream, breathing heavily. She placed her hand to her throat. No necklace, but she felt a strange, pulsing warmth, as though the gem had been resting against her skin.

"Prue, are you all right?"

Startled by the familiar but unexpected voice, she gasped as Robert turned on her lamp. He stood in front of her desk, his gaze intense as he studied her.

"Are you all right?" he repeated.

Frowning, she nodded. "Yes, I just . . . drifted off for a minute. I knew it was getting dark. I don't know why I didn't turn on my lamp."

"You work too hard," Robert said quietly as he set a bottle on her desk.

"What's that?" she asked.

"The champagne from New Year's Eve. I know it's probably gone flat by now. But it was bought for you. I thought you might at least want the bottle—as a souvenir."

Old, flat champagne, Prue thought. Could a gift get any less romantic? Especially if she compared it to the kisses of her midnight phantom. She wanted to return to the dream. She resented Robert's showing up, stopping her from basking in the glow of its aftermath.

"I don't want this," she told him—and immediately saw the hurt in his eyes.

Why did I say that? she wondered with a sense of remorse. He only offered me a gift. I could have taken it and thrown it away later. I didn't have to hurt him.

She suddenly realized that she *wanted* to hurt him. She wanted him out of her office and out of her life. Robert Galliard was of no use to her.

"What are you doing here anyway?" she demanded impatiently.

"I had some business with Claire and decided to stop by your office. You haven't returned my phone calls," he added a bit defensively.

She straightened the papers on her desk. "I've been busy. Like you said, I work too hard."

"I left a message about taking you to the theater on Friday night—"

"I already have plans," she said quickly.

"I see. So your business schedule and your personal schedule are completely filled up."

As far as you're concerned, she thought. Yes.

She pressed her fingers to her temples. Where had that ugly thought come from? She wasn't attracted to Robert anymore, but he didn't deserve this kind of attitude.

"Robert"—she forced herself to sound polite—"I don't mean to sound so harsh, but I really don't see us going anywhere."

"Not even as friends?"

A surge of anger rose from inside Prue. Part of her wanted to spare Robert's feelings, but part of her wanted to be rid of him forever. It made no sense. He's a nice guy, she thought. Why do I dislike him more every time I see him?

Because he's pathetic, she thought. He knows you don't want him and he keeps persisting. He's begging you. He's disgusting.

Prue shuddered and glanced at Robert. She didn't really think he was pathetic, did she?

Robert's gaze settled on her, and she wished she could look away, but his eyes pleaded for her to listen.

"Prue, in a few days the paperwork will be complete, and I'll get the necklace from Claiborne. Then I must return to Paris. But first I thought we could have dinner. You know—to celebrate my latest acquisition, to make up for the way New Year's Eve turned out."

Prue stared at him. This was too much of a coincidence, she thought. First I dreamed about the midnight phantom and the necklace, and now Robert is standing here, talking about the very same piece of jewelry.

In the deepest recesses of her mind, Prue knew something odd was going on. Are you the stranger I've been so obsessed with? she wondered. Are you the one who kissed me at midnight on New Year's Eve?

No, she thought, remembering the sweetness of Robert's mouth against hers. His kiss didn't even come close. And yet she knew that if Robert had kissed her before the phantom, it wouldn't have even occurred to her that he was second rate.

Prue's mind spun with confusion. I need to get out of here, she thought frantically. I need to think things through and put them in perspective. She shoved back her chair and got to her feet. "I have a meeting to attend."

Robert scowled at her obvious lie. "At this time of night? I was hoping I could take you to dinner."

"I thought you wanted to go to dinner when you got the necklace."

"Then *and* now. There is so much I want to talk to you about," he said. He sounded so sincere that he almost convinced her to say yes.

But she knew that would be the wrong answer. The wrong path. Something about Robert creeped her out. She couldn't explain it. She shook her head. "I have to meet with a client."

She grabbed her briefcase and walked out of her office.

"Prue!" he called after her.

Ignoring him, she quickened her pace. I don't like the way he keeps after me, she thought. I should have to say no only once.

She walked out of the Buckland's building, got into her car, and started driving. She didn't know where she was going, but it didn't matter. It felt good to be alone.

Images began to bombard her mind:

Robert.

The man in her dreams, always hidden in shadows.

The necklace, glowing with emerald fire.

A kiss of passion, a kiss of life.

She felt a wave of dizziness, and an unexpected heat swirl through her. Quickly she pulled off the road, afraid she'd wind up in accident.

She tried to think about Robert calmly, rationally, but the thoughts were pushed back by panic messages.

He's dangerous! something inside her screamed. Where is this stuff coming from? she wondered.

As if in answer, a vision of the man from her dreams emerged. And then all she could think about was the rush that went through her when his lips touched hers.

She thought of his gift—the necklace that Robert had come to San Francisco for, the necklace he would soon have.

She was sure Robert was not the phantom. But why were both he and the man in her dreams connected to the emerald necklace?

CHAPTER
7

That night Prue rolled over in bed and felt his presence again—the midnight phantom.

He was with her, filling her mind, delighting her body. It seemed as though he were flesh and blood, standing with her beyond the boundaries of any real world.

They were at Lloyd Claiborne's again, and the necklace was around her neck, the emerald growing warm and pulsing just below her throat.

Without hesitation, he covered her mouth with his completely, absolutely. The wonder of his kiss amazed her.

How could any man kiss with such raw power? How could any woman resist him?

He drew away, his face, as always, hidden by shadows. She wanted to reach out and touch his jaw, his cheek. To know he was real, that he was more than a figment of her imagination.

He covered the emerald necklace with his palm. The heat increased and a sharp green light shot out from beneath his hand.

Prue shut her eyes against the brightness that threatened to blind her.

She felt him move his hands up until he placed them just above the necklace at the base of her throat. His hands caressed her soft skin, sending shivers through her body.

Then his fingers tightened, digging into her neck, his thumbs pressing against her windpipe.

Panic shot through her as he squeezed tighter, crushing her throat, cutting off her air. She heard a harsh ringing in her ears, and blood thrummed at her temples. Her eyes bulged as she gasped for air.

His hands became cold, like death, and her body became weak. But she didn't fall. The midnight phantom held her upright, his hands closing around her throat. Tighter . . . tighter . . .

Prue jerked awake, frightened and disoriented.

Breathing heavily, she touched her neck lightly and glanced around. The morning light eased through the window of her bedroom.

Her bedroom. She was safe in her own room.

"So it was just a nightmare," she murmured. But she knew it was more than that. It was too vivid, too real. The man in her dreams had tried to murder her. Almost as disturbing, he'd taken as much pleasure in her terror as he took in her kisses.

She shuddered. No more. Her mysterious phantom had turned evil. She wouldn't—couldn't—think about him anymore, and if she didn't think about him, she wouldn't dream about him.

"Oh, no!" She glanced at her clock and bolted out of bed. She'd overslept. She had exactly forty-five minutes to get to Buckland's to prepare for a major Saturday auction. Claire would kill her if she was late—or, worse, fire her.

She took a quick shower, wishing it didn't have to be so hurried. The stream of hot water felt wonderful, reviving her, clearing away the remaining cobwebs of her nightmare.

As Prue got dressed, her mind circled back to the midnight phantom. All right. So she couldn't banish him from her thoughts so easily. *I feel like he's part of me,* she thought. *And the truth is, I still want him.*

Feeling shaky, Prue sat down on the edge of the bed. This wasn't like her. Prue Halliwell was practical, clearheaded, and cool about guys, definitely not the type to obsess. Especially about a man she dreamed wanted to kill her.

So what am I doing? she asked herself. *Or what is it that I should do?*

What she really wanted was to find out who the mysterious man was, because even after the nightmare, she wanted him firmly in the middle of her reality.

Prue thought about Claiborne's New Year's Eve party and wondered if there was a way to get a copy of the guest list. Maybe Lloyd Claiborne would show up at today's auction and she could ask some very casual questions.

Feeling a little better now that she had a plan, she sprayed on some perfume and sniffed her wrist.

No scent.

This perfume must be old, she thought, and tossed it into the wastebasket.

She picked up another bottle and dabbed some of it on. She inhaled deeply. Again no fragrance. She threw that one out too, thinking, I don't have time for this.

She sprayed on a third fragrance before she hurriedly finished dressing.

Phoebe walked into the kitchen, surprised to see Piper staring at the newspaper, nearly catatonic. She looks as though someone died, Phoebe thought. Her mind raced to Billy. Please let him be all right, she silently prayed.

"What's wrong?" Phoebe asked, her concern increasing as she got a closer look at her sister.

"Everything," Piper said. She groaned and tossed the newspaper across the table.

Phoebe stared at the front page. In full color, a large photo showed a woman from the neck down, wearing only the top of a purple gown, her skirt wrapped around her ankles. "Unknown woman steals the scene," she read the headline aloud in disgust. "I can't believe what some people do to get attention."

Piper groaned again, and Phoebe glanced away from the paper to see her sister's shattered expression.

"Phoebe, that's me," Piper said.

Phoebe jerked her gaze back to the photo. The purple top, the purple swath of skirt. Oh, my goodness, she thought, recognizing what remained of the beautiful gown Piper had ordered.

"What happened?" Phoebe asked.

"Some woman stepped on the hem of my skirt. She stopped walking—Jake and I didn't. My skirt stayed with the woman. I've never been so humiliated in my entire life!"

Phoebe winced in sympathy. "What did you do?"

"What *could* I do? I froze time. Then I set a record for sprinting in four-inch heels." Piper buried her head in her arms. "How am I ever going to face Jake again?"

"I take it Jake doesn't know what happened," Phoebe said.

"I don't think so. Flashbulbs were going off, and his eyes were closed when I stopped time. When he opened them again, I was gone. Poof! Like a cloud of smoke."

"You need to call him and sort things out," Phoebe said in a rational voice.

Piper lifted her head. "I don't know if I can do that. What do I tell him?"

"The truth." Phoebe held up a hand. "Except for the freezing-time part. It's too much for him this early in your relationship, but he should be able to accept and forgive the rest. If he can't, then he's not worth your energy."

"Thanks. That's really helpful." Piper gave a sigh of profound misery. "It's just that I really like this guy. And every time we get together, something goes majorly wrong."

"That's not the only thing that's going wrong around here," Phoebe murmured.

"What do you mean?" Piper asked.

Phoebe hesitated, afraid she'd sound as though she'd gone nuts. But she had to tell someone even though she knew Prue wouldn't welcome her suspicions. "I think Robert might have put a love spell on Prue."

"Excuse me? Where did you get this idea?"

Phoebe narrowed her eyes. "New Year's, he told me that he had tried *everything* to make Prue like him, and that it hadn't turned out the way he expected."

"And you think *everything* is a love spell?"

"He poured Prue's champagne back into the bottle and took it with him, which I find just a little odd," Phoebe pointed out. "Like maybe he didn't want anyone else to drink it."

"That is a bit weird," Piper admitted. "But I wouldn't accuse Robert because of that."

"I know. That's why I went to *The Book of Shadows*. I found a love spell that requires a potion. And don't forget, Prue's kissing bug started on New Year's Eve. I tried to ask her about it last night, but she was too busy smooching with the pizza delivery guy," Phoebe said.

"Well, if you're right, I think it's kind of cute that Robert would go to the trouble of trying a love spell," Piper said.

"*Cute?*" Phoebe cried. "Don't you see? If Robert has access to magic, he's part of *our world*," she said. "Maybe he's even a warlock."

She watched Piper's mouth drop open. "You know, there could be other explanations," Piper said. "After all, Robert deals in antiques. Maybe he ran across an old spell book and decided to give it a try."

"I suppose that's possible," Phoebe said. "If that's the case, I'd like to see the book."

Phoebe spun around as Prue sailed into the kitchen, reeking of perfume. Did she take a bath in the stuff? Phoebe wondered.

"I'm just going to grab some coffee. I'm late for work," Prue announced.

Phoebe coughed and waved at the air in front of her. "Don't you think your perfume is just a little heavy this morning?"

"I can't smell a thing."

She can't smell a thing? Phoebe repeated to herself, on the verge of gagging as she watched Prue take a sip of coffee.

"It was weird though," Prue continued. "For some reason, all my perfume decided to expire this morning. I tried three different bottles and none of them had any fragrance." She put the empty coffee mug back on the counter and started out of the kitchen. "Later."

Phoebe watched Prue hurry out of the house,

then turned to Piper. "Did you smell what I did?"

Piper nodded, tears welling in her eyes. "My eyes are still stinging. I can't believe Prue didn't smell it."

"Either she's getting sick, or whatever Robert did is not affecting only her common sense but her nose," Phoebe answered. "I think it's time we put an end to this love spell."

Piper laughed. "Definitely. Before Prue asphyxiates us all."

Coming down the stairs that evening, Piper heard the sound of a motorcycle roaring to a stop. She peered out the window and gasped.

"What are you looking at?" Phoebe asked, walking toward her.

"You're not going to believe this, but I think Prue just joined a gang," Piper said. "I know, this morning I wasn't ready to believe Robert had put a love spell on Prue, but someone sure has done something to change her taste in men."

"What are you talking about?" Phoebe asked. She looked out the window and gasped. "He looks like a jewelry box exploded onto his face."

Piper nodded, still unable to believe her eyes.

Prue stood in the front yard, making out with a burly guy with a shaved head. He wore so many dangling earrings and chains that Piper wondered how his ears stayed attached to his head. Pierced eyebrows, nose, lips—

"Where does she find them?" Piper murmured.

"It doesn't matter," Phoebe said. "This has got to stop."

"I agree." She and Phoebe waited by the door until Prue finally came in. But Prue didn't look pleased or excited or any of the things you might expect after kissing a guy. She just looked puzzled.

"Hot kiss?" Piper asked.

"Until the end," Prue admitted, sounding distracted. "Now I wish I'd never kissed him."

"No kidding," Piper said. "You have to stop kissing total strangers."

"I know!" Prue said impatiently. "I tried to explain it to you at the park. I can't control this urge I get." She placed a hand to her forehead. "I don't know what's happening to me!"

"We think Robert put a love spell on you," Phoebe blurted out.

Prue's eyes widened. "Robert? A love spell? You can't be serious."

"I didn't want to believe it either," Piper said. "But he told Phoebe that he'd done something to make you like him and it didn't work. So we figure . . . love spell."

"I don't know, but something weird is definitely going on," Prue admitted.

"I say we cast a counterspell and then we confront Robert," Phoebe said. "Just to cover our bases."

Prue shook her head. "I'm all for the counterspell, but if you're suggesting Robert is a warlock, I can't buy that. I've known him for over a year.

Besides, if he put a spell on me and it didn't work, he would have done something else by now."

"So maybe it wasn't Robert," Piper said, doubts surfacing. She tried to think of another possibility. But nothing came to her. "We can figure out who's responsible later," she said. "Right now we need to get this spell off you."

Prue held up a hand. Piper was surprised to see it shaking. "If there is a spell, I want it gone. I didn't tell either of you this, but something happens after I kiss someone. His face changes. I—I see him dying. I want to stop kissing these men, but . . . I can't. All I can think about is finding the next kiss. It's starting to scare me."

"This definitely sounds like some sort of spell," Phoebe said. "Let's get to *The Book of Shadows*."

Piper led the way up the stairs to the attic. "Phoebe looked through the book earlier," she told Prue. "She found a couple of spells that we think will remove the original one."

"Use the strongest one," Prue urged them.

"What if it makes you never want to kiss a guy again?" Piper asked.

Prue gave her a wry smile. "Right now that doesn't sound like such a bad tradeoff."

In the attic, Phoebe stood before the podium that held *The Book of Shadows*. She turned to the page that she and Piper had marked earlier.

"It's going to take the Power of Three," Piper said. "This silly spell has no chance if we don't link our powers together."

"Let's do it," Prue told her.

Phoebe moved away from the book. She took a piece of chalk from her pocket and used it to draw a circle on the floor.

"Hold hands," Phoebe said.

Piper felt her mouth go dry. She always worried that they'd mess up the spell.

"Close your eyes," Phoebe ordered, "and repeat after me three times, 'The power of love comes from the heart/The desire to kiss is but a start/Remove the spell to separate the two/Remove the spell placed on Prue.' "

Piper closed her eyes and tightened her hold on each of her sister's hands. She heard her sisters' voices mingle with hers as she chanted the words: "The power of love comes from the heart/The desire to kiss is but a start/Remove the spell that separates the two/Remove the spell placed on Prue."

Amazed, Piper felt a sudden chill rise up from the floor. It came into her, shimmering up her legs, up her body. She heard her heart pounding, and a trickle of fear raced through her.

Please let this be the correct spell, she thought, and please let us do it right.

She felt both Prue's and Phoebe's hands tremble in hers and knew they were experiencing the cold as well.

As one, they repeated the words to break the love spell.

Suddenly a wind whipped up like a tornado around the circle. It surrounded them, howling.

Piper tried not to be distracted by the storm.

She forced herself to concentrate on the chant, and she knew her sisters did the same, because she saw their lips moving. But all she could hear was the roaring of the wind.

Piper felt Phoebe's grip tighten around her hand and then felt Prue's do the same. It's going to work, she thought to herself. Everything's going to be all right.

Thunder rumbled, the floor trembled, and heat suddenly swept through Piper. She felt fire and ice battling within her. The wind screeched.

Then silence.

Piper still heard the ringing in her ears, but the wind had vanished. Her body tingled. "Is it over?" she whispered.

Phoebe nodded. "I think so."

Piper turned to Prue. "How do you feel?"

Prue glanced slowly around the room, her voice trembling when she spoke. "Okay, I guess."

"Do you need to kiss anyone?" Piper asked hesitantly.

Prue licked her lips before pressing them together. "No."

Piper squeezed her hand. "So you think we managed to break the spell?"

Prue nodded. "Definitely. No more kisses for me."

"At least for a while," Phoebe suggested.

Prue released their hands and backed up a step. "As far as I'm concerned, it can be forever."

CHAPTER
8

Sitting on the living room floor, Phoebe sketched out different ideas for Quake's stationery. Nothing seemed right.

You're trying too hard, she silently reprimanded herself. Just relax and it'll come.

She'd had the same problem when she'd first discovered her power of premonition. If she concentrated on trying to see things, nothing ever happened. In the beginning she tried so hard that she gave herself migraine headaches, until she finally accepted both the limitations and the magnitude of her power.

The premonitions came when she least expected them.

So would the perfect image for Quake's stationery.

She had sketched Quake's logo in the corner—

a broken boulder, supposedly from a real earthquake. The letters *QUA* were chiseled on one half of the stone and the letters *KE* on the other.

Phoebe redrew the logo a little larger. Then, using acrylic paints, she tried to come up with some kind of great background design. Gradually she began to relax, getting lost in the colors and texture of the paint.

She glanced up as the front door opened. Piper shuffled in, her shoulders slumped. Phoebe didn't need her psychic power to know something was wrong.

"What's happened?" she asked, shoving the paper and paints aside.

Piper dropped onto the floor beside her. "Since it's my night off from Quake, I thought I'd stop by the hospital and see Billy. I cooked his favorite meal and took it to him. He said he couldn't taste it. He wouldn't eat it." Tears welled in her eyes, and she covered her mouth. "His skin is all shriveled. He looks like a skeleton lying in that bed. I'm afraid he's going to die."

Phoebe put her arms around her sister and drew her close. "He'll be all right," Phoebe said, not sure she believed it herself.

Piper shook her head. "This disease is like something from a horror movie where a virus destroys the entire world. Billy's whole ward is full of people with the same sickness. At first they thought the virus was limited to people from Lloyd Claiborne's parties and Quake. Now other people have been admitted. It's spreading."

"So if it's not something exclusive to Quake's or Claiborne's parties," Phoebe said, "there must be something else all these people have in common."

Piper stared at the floor. "Probably. But Billy can't tell us what it is. He kept moving his mouth, and I knew he wanted to say something to me, but his voice was so weak, I could barely hear him." She sniffed, and tears rolled down her cheeks.

Phoebe hugged Piper more tightly. "The doctors will figure out what's going on."

"They'd better figure it out soon," Piper said in a grim tone. "They know it's not food poisoning. But so far no one can determine exactly what's wrong with Billy or how to stop it. One doctor said it's as if all these people are just fading away . . . for no reason."

"At least no one has died," Phoebe reminded her.

Piper sat up and seemed a bit calmer. "Do you know who I saw going into the hospital? The guy who delivered my dress."

Phoebe felt a cold shiver race through her. It was bad enough that Billy was in the hospital, but to think that someone else they knew was in there as well . . . "Maybe he was going to visit someone who was sick," she said optimistically.

"I don't think so. He was pale and fell to the floor before they got to him."

"Oh." She tried to think of something a little more cheerful to say to get Piper's mind off the hospital. "How is Jake doing?"

"Jake?"

Phoebe nudged her arm. "Yes, Jake. What did he say when you called to apologize about the premiere?"

Piper looked away with guilt.

"You didn't call him, did you?" Phoebe asked.

"I didn't know what to say." Piper leaned back against the leg of the table. "Every explanation I came up with sounded so stupid and unbelievable."

Phoebe sighed. She knew Piper was making a mistake with Jake, but she couldn't tell her sister how to live her life. She reached for the pad of paper that she'd been working on. "I've been trying to come up with something really different for your stationery." She showed Piper the pad. "What do you think?"

Piper narrowed her eyes. She opened her mouth to speak, then closed it.

"You don't like it," Phoebe said.

"It's not that," Piper said hesitantly. "It's just . . . how did you come up with this?"

"I don't know," Phoebe said. "I just relaxed and it kind of popped into my head."

Piper nibbled on her lower lip. "You know what your background reminds me of? That creepy card from Prue's tarot reading. The one with the black tower and all those symbols."

Phoebe took the pad and looked at her drawings more closely. Piper was right. "It must have made a bigger impression on me than I thought." She touched a finger to one of the geometric shapes she had painted behind the Quake logo.

Bright light flashed into Phoebe's eyes. A quick jolt of electricity raced through her body. She gasped, overcome with fear but recognizing the sign of an impending vision. She closed her eyes, waiting for the scene to unfold in her mind:

A tarot card. Waving back and forth.

The black tower. The card that had frightened Elena.

And Elena. Here. In the house. In the attic.

Prue. Lying on the floor.

Elena waving the card over her. Chanting.

Words. Phoebe couldn't make out the words!

Prue! Poor Prue!

Her body withered, skin stretched taut.

Her lips blackened, cracked, and bleeding.

Her face, a grayish hue. Her eyes sunken.

Trying to speak, gasping for air.

Fighting for breath.

Fighting to live—and losing!

Phoebe moaned in anguish. Her mind whirling. The images disappeared, and she bowed her head against the dizziness.

"Hey." Piper touched Phoebe's shoulders. "Phebes, are you okay?" she asked.

Phoebe *wasn't* okay, but she couldn't answer. Tears stung the backs of her eyes, and a thick lump rose inside her throat.

How could I ever be okay? she wondered, her heart pounding. Prue is going to die!

CHAPTER
9

Piper gazed at her sister, worried. Phoebe was pale, her head lowered. "Phoebe, what's wrong?" she asked. "I didn't mean to hurt your feelings. I like the brightness of your design, but those symbols from the tarot card . . ." She shook her head. "It's just not right for Quake."

Phoebe didn't answer, she just kept staring at the pad of paper.

Why didn't I just keep my mouth shut? Piper wondered. Phoebe can get so sensitive about things when she tries so hard and we criticize her. She touched Phoebe's arm. "Phoebe, don't get upset over this. I know you'll come up with something better, something that will work—"

The phone rang, and Piper nearly jumped out of her skin.

"Get the phone," Phoebe whispered, distracted, her gaze still focused on the paper.

Piper got up and grabbed the receiver. "Hello?"

"Hey, remember me?"

Her heart did a little twist, a turn, and she smiled for the first time all day. She turned her back on Phoebe for a little privacy. "Hi, Jake."

"So, you do remember. I wasn't sure if you would."

Piper cringed at the doubts she heard in his voice.

"The strangest thing happened to me the other night," he went on. "I took a beautiful woman to a premiere. I looked away for one second, and when I looked back, she was gone. Like David Copperfield. Poof! Magic. She disappeared. What happened, Piper? Why did you leave?"

Piper winced at the hurt she heard in his voice. "Oh, Jake, I'm so sorry."

"I felt like a jerk, Piper. If you didn't want to go, all you had to do was tell me."

"But I *did* want to go. Something came up and I had to leave. I didn't know what to say. . . ."

"How's Billy?" Jake asked. Piper thought she heard irritation in his voice.

"He's so sick, Jake," Piper told him. "I'm practically *living* at the hospital."

"Are you sure there isn't something going on between the two of you?" he asked.

"What do you mean?" Piper asked a little annoyed. "He's really sick. He's my friend. That's all."

"I'm sorry," Jake said. "I know you told me you two were close. I just didn't know what to think after you disappeared on me though."

"I can explain," she offered. "A woman stepped on my skirt, and you and I kept walking. My skirt stayed behind. I'm sorry, but I had to get out of there. Didn't you see the newspaper the next morning?"

"I don't usually get around to reading the paper," Jake answered. "But I'm sorry I missed it," he added with a laugh.

"I'm not," she said in a small voice. "It was so humiliating."

Jake laughed again. "I guess I would have run too," he admitted.

"I'm sorry I didn't call you to explain. I hope someday you'll give me another chance," Piper said, crossing her fingers as she held the phone.

"I was hoping you would ·give *me* another chance," he said. "How about tomorrow afternoon?"

Joy shot through her. "Tomorrow? That would be perfect!"

"Great. Meet me at the Presidio at three for a picnic."

Piper hung up, feeling a little giddy. She was so glad Jake had taken another chance on her. This time she was going to make sure everything went right.

She turned, and her sudden happiness fled. Phoebe was bent over her design, frantically trying to paint over the symbols she'd created earlier. But the strange geometric shapes seemed to reemerge through the layers of paint, as though nothing could hide them, nothing could stop them now that they'd been created.

Piper knelt beside her sister. "Phoebe?" she asked. "What are you doing? What's going on?"

Phoebe didn't say anything.

Piper grabbed her sister's shoulders and pulled her upright. "Tell me," she said. "What's wrong with you?"

"I—I had a vision," Phoebe stammered. "I saw Prue. She was lying on the floor—dying! Elena, the tarot reader, was waving a card over her—the one with the black tower." Phoebe shifted her gaze from Piper back to the symbols in her design. "I think I might have been wrong—or if I wasn't wrong, I wasn't right enough. Robert might have put a love spell on Prue, but something else is going on too. I don't know exactly what, but it has to do with Elena, that tower card, and Prue dying!"

"How?" Piper tried to make sense with what Phoebe was saying, but she couldn't. "Why would Elena do that? She's just a tarot reader. She doesn't even know us."

"We can't be sure of that," Phoebe countered. "We're the Charmed Ones, remember? Elena's not exactly going to tell us she's a warlock."

Piper felt a sickening jolt of dread go through her. "You're right, Phoebe. We have no way of knowing who to trust." She placed a comforting hand on her sister's shoulder. "Okay. Let's calm down. We'll figure something out."

Piper gasped, startled, when Prue burst through the front door, carrying an armload of groceries. She was both relieved to see Prue looking fairly normal, and worried that Phoebe's vision would come true anyway—as her visions always did.

Piper tried to keep her voice casual. "So, how are you feeling?"

"Great," Prue answered. "Actually I was wondering if you both wanted to see a movie tonight."

"You're going to take us to a movie?" Phoebe asked.

"No, but I'll treat if you want to go," Prue offered.

Suspicious, Piper studied her older sister. "Why are you so eager for us to see a movie?"

A dreamy expression swept over Prue's face. "I just met the most incredible guy, and I invited him for dinner. He'll be here in half an hour, so I need you two out of the house." She started across the room, then stopped.

Piper saw Prue's gaze fall to the sketchpad on the floor.

"What's this?" Prue asked.

"Phoebe is designing some stationery for Quake," Piper explained.

Prue snatched up the pad. "You really expect Quake to use this?" she asked Phoebe. "You couldn't get the design right if you used a paint-by-numbers kit."

"Thanks a lot!" Phoebe replied, trying not to

look hurt. "It's so nice to get encouragement from your family."

Prue didn't answer but marched toward the kitchen, taking the pad with her.

"Everyone's an art critic!" Phoebe said bitterly.

"No," Piper disagreed. "Prue would never be that mean."

Phoebe gave a weary sigh. "It's obvious the counterspell didn't work. She's still chasing after guys, and now she's being hateful too."

"That's not the worst of it." Piper exchanged a panicked look with her sister. "How are we going to stop your vision from coming true?"

Tossing some pasta into boiling water, Prue thought about Eugene. She'd been waiting at a stoplight and had looked over at the car next to her. The driver was beating his hands on the steering wheel in rhythm to some music blasting from his radio. He'd smiled at her. He had a beautiful mouth. She'd rolled down her window and invited him to dinner.

It was so easy, she thought. Why hadn't she ever done this before?

The doorbell rang. Excitement shot through her. He was early. "I'll get it," she called.

She walked through the living room. Piper and Phoebe were still there, clearly refusing to leave.

Fine, Prue thought. They can do what they want. They won't stop me from doing what I want.

She opened the door, and her smile faded. Robert stood on the porch.

"Hello, Prue."

"What are you doing here?" she asked.

"I couldn't get hold of you," he replied. "I really wanted to see you, Prue."

"I've been busy," she said coldly. "You know how it is at Buckland's."

He gave her a small nod. "Yes, I know how it can be at times."

I don't want you here, she thought. You're of no use to me.

He stepped over the threshold, but Prue refused to step back, blocking him from entering the house.

"Prue," he said softly. Reaching out, he touched her cheek.

She recoiled, repulsed. "Don't touch me!" she cried. "You have no right!"

"What did I do to make you dislike me?" Robert asked gently.

Prue tried to think of an answer, but nothing came to mind. I don't have a clue, she realized. She knew only that he was a threat to her—especially after Phoebe found out about the spell he tried to place on her.

She stared at him coldly. "I don't dislike you," she said, forcing out the words.

Robert tried again. "I'm sorry for stopping by on such short notice, but I just had a business dinner canceled. I was wondering if I could take you out this evening."

Prue studied his stance, wondering why he kept persisting. She thought she'd made it obvious that she had no interest in going out with him. What made him think she'd change her mind? Had he really cast a spell on her? A wicked thought occurred to her. If he had, maybe the spell had worked in reverse and made him love her, not her love him.

She rubbed her forehead, feeling a headache coming on. "I don't understand, Robert. Why do you keep asking me out? Why don't you just give up?"

With a confident grin, he leaned toward her. "Because you're in love with me," he told her. "You just haven't realized it yet."

The words made Prue's stomach sour. He still thinks I'm under his spell, she thought. "You couldn't be more wrong," she told him. She pressed her palm against his solid chest and shoved him back through the door onto the porch. "Good night!"

"Prue—"

She shut the door.

"Prue, open the door!" he shouted.

"In your dreams," she muttered, and started back toward the kitchen. She was certain now that Robert *wasn't* a warlock. Would a warlock let himself be pushed out the door? No. As Piper said, he probably had tried a love spell in a book and got it wrong.

She glanced at her watch. Robert's little visit had thrown her off schedule. She wanted the food on the table, candles lit, and wine poured by the time Eugene arrived.

She staggered slightly as she passed through the living room and grabbed for a chair. Her legs felt strange—a little shaky.

Phoebe glanced up from the couch. "Are you all right?" she asked.

"I'm fine," Prue snapped, "but I'd feel a lot finer if you and Piper would get out of my face!"

Phoebe held up her hands. "I'll go to my room when your hot date gets here. Or was that him at the door?"

"No, it was Robert."

"What did he want?" Phoebe asked, genuine concern in her voice.

"Maybe he wanted to cast another spell. I don't know and I don't care. He's not what *I* want!" she yelled.

Phoebe looked at her with a stunned expression.

Prue raised her hand to her chest, trying to calm down and catch her breath. Robert, Phoebe, Piper, she thought. They're all in my way. They're all trying to ruin my evening.

She closed her eyes and inhaled deeply, then slowly made her way to the kitchen. I'm losing control, she thought, not used to feeling that way. Maybe I really am working too hard. What else could explain why I'm so exhausted and moody lately? Poor Eugene. All he was going to get tonight was dinner and a kiss.

She held on to the kitchen counter, again needing to steady herself. Maybe I'm coming down with a cold, she thought.

An image of Eugene flashed into her mind, and her lips tingled. She needed his kiss as much as she needed to breathe. And he was so cute, with an exceptionally nice, lean, muscled body.

She wanted a passionate kiss that would make her senses reel, a kiss like the one she'd had at midnight on New Year's Eve. Especially because this time there would be no horrifying visions of someone dying. This time the spell was broken.

Prue pushed herself away from the counter, dropped butter into a skillet, and turned the flame on. She grabbed a large chopping knife and began to dice onions and garlic for the sauce.

She heard the butter begin to sizzle and lowered the flame. She stared at the onion and garlic. She couldn't smell either one—or the butter, for that matter.

She added chopped zucchini and peppers to the pan and heard the hiss as cold met hot. She stirred them, but still no scent.

She reached for a Portobello mushroom, sliced it, then dropped it into the skillet. She stirred the vegetables and butter but still couldn't smell anything. Maybe I didn't use enough onions and garlic, she thought.

Impatient she peeled another clove of garlic and began to chop furiously. How could garlic not smell? Had she bought stale ingredients?

"What are you doing, Prue?" Piper asked from the doorway. "Trying to ward off vampires?"

Prue's eyes widened in alarm. "You can smell the garlic?"

"Of course I can smell it. The whole house reeks of it."

"Then why can't *I* smell anything?"

"You're getting a cold?" Piper guessed.

Prue turned to face her sister. "I have been feeling kind of run-down."

Then Piper gasped and ran to Prue's side. "What did you do?" Piper cried, grabbing Prue's hand.

Feeling detached, Prue watched a stream of bright red blood run from a wide cut that crossed her palm. Blood dripped onto the knife, the counter, and the garlic.

She felt dizzy as she caught sight of the dark red stains on her clothes. Why don't I feel any pain? she wondered. I didn't even realize I was hurt.

"Prue!" Piper wrapped a sheath of paper towels around her hand and pressed hard. "We've got to stop the bleeding."

Prue didn't answer. She was strangely fascinated by the way her blood soaked through the paper towels. Blood dripped from the towels into the pan. Prue watched it sizzle. "That's better," she said with a smile of satisfaction.

"What is?" Piper asked.

"I think I can smell the blood burning," she replied.

CHAPTER
10

Phoebe glanced up from the couch to see Piper helping Prue out of the kitchen.

"What's wrong?" she asked, pushing back her chair and getting up.

"Prue just needs to lie down," Piper answered quickly over the sound of the doorbell. "Can you get the door and tell Romeo his date is off?"

For a moment Phoebe stared after her sisters as Piper helped Prue up the stairs, wondering exactly what was going on. Then she walked to the front door and jerked it open.

Her breath caught at the sight of the young man on their porch. He had a strong, muscular build, but he was even younger than the skateboarder. He gave her a silly grin, and she had a feeling he'd never had a date before.

"Is the girl with the black hair here?" he asked.

Shocked, Phoebe glared at him. "The girl with the black hair? You don't know her name?"

"Nope. She just invited me to dinner, and, hey, I'm always ready to eat. You know what I mean?"

"Yes, I think I do," Phoebe said, trying to be polite. "I'm sorry, but she's not feeling well."

"Bummer." He shrugged. "Guess I could eat with you," he said, starting into the house.

Phoebe put the tip of her finger against his chest and pushed him back. "I don't think so."

He looked at her curiously. "There's a new Hong Kong kung fu movie playing in Chinatown," he told her. "Wanna go?"

"No," Phoebe told him.

Oh," he said, sounding disappointed. He flashed her that goofy smile. "Maybe some other time."

She closed the door and watched him through the window, walking off, confused over Prue's choice in men lately.

Phoebe sat down in one of the wicker chairs to think. She was sure that something more than a love spell gone wrong was at work here. She looked up at the sound of footsteps coming down the stairs, and her heart tightened at the grim expression on Piper's face.

"What happened?" Phoebe asked.

Piper pursed her lips. "Prue cut herself making dinner."

"Does she need stitches?"

"No, but I think something is seriously wrong with her," Piper answered. "She was trembling, but I don't think it was because of the gash. Then she fell asleep as soon as her head hit the pillow."

"Okay, I'll call a doctor." Phoebe grabbed the phone book. Several phone calls later, she slammed down the receiver. "Every doctor I called is booked solid. No one can see Prue for at least two weeks. They suggest we take her to an emergency room."

Piper sighed. "Prue is sound asleep right now. I don't think whatever is going on really warrants a trip to the hospital."

"That's good," Phoebe said. "Hospitals make me nervous."

Piper pulled her zippered sweatshirt closed. "Actually, trying to get her in to see a doctor was probably a dumb idea. I have a feeling that whatever is wrong with Prue isn't something modern medicine can cure."

"Good point," Phoebe agreed quickly. "Which means we need more information—of the non-medical kind."

Piper sat cross-legged on the couch. "Maybe we're dealing with two spells," she suggested. "Maybe they became intertwined somehow."

Phoebe shook her head. "Realistically what are the odds that two spells are going to be put on one witch? No, I think it's something simpler. Something we've never seen before. And until we know what we're dealing with, I think we're only asking for trouble if we use another counterspell. Maybe we should start with the one piece of information that we do have."

"What's that?"

"My vision," Phoebe reminded her. "You know, Elena waving the tarot card."

"I don't want to leave Prue right now," Piper said, looking toward the second floor. "I want to be here in case she needs anything. But tomorrow I'll go to the Railyard Café to see what I can find out about Elena. Then I'll try Giovanni's. Prue said they catered Claiborne's party, and we know Elena was there too. Maybe one of the waiters can tell me what exactly went on that night."

Phoebe got to her feet. "Sounds like a plan. If we're going to be here, let's take another look at *The Book of Shadows*. Maybe we'll find something on that tarot card."

"Good idea," Piper said.

Phoebe followed Piper up the stairs to the attic. Together they crossed the room to the podium where *The Book of Shadows* rested. "Here goes," Phoebe said, folding back the leather cover.

She began skimming through the pages. It wasn't an easy thing to do, since the book had been handwritten by many Halliwell ancestors over the years. Some of the pages were written in a formal, elaborate script so different from contemporary handwriting that it was almost illegible. On other pages the handwriting was so tiny and cramped that you practically needed a magnifying glass to decipher it.

Phoebe turned the pages until an illustration stopped her. It was a sketch of a strikingly handsome man with dark hair. But his eyes—something in his blue eyes spoke of evil.

"Piper, look at this," she said, trying to keep her voice calm. "Do you notice anything familiar about him?" Phoebe asked.

Piper stepped closer and studied the drawing. "Not really," she replied.

Phoebe shook her head and touched the robe he wore. "Look at the pattern on his robe. It's got the same symbols that were on that tarot card. The same pattern I subconsciously drew on the stationery for Quake."

Piper pointed to the text below the picture. "Looks as if somebody wrote this in a hurry. Can you make out what it says?"

Phoebe felt her heart speed up and the blood pulse in her temples as she tried to decipher the words. "I think this page is a warning," she said at last. "About this guy. The first sentence reads, 'Lascaris was a powerful warlock who arrived in France in the late 1700s.' "

"A warlock," Piper repeated sarcastically. "Why am I not surprised? What else does it say?"

" 'He would charm young women and have them collect his life force by kissing men. He needed the strength of these men to keep him young and virile for centuries.' "

"Kissing," Piper repeated. "We're definitely onto something."

Phoebe winced as she read the next sentence. "'He was obsessed with a particular deck of tarot cards and used them to predict his victims—the ones on whom his spells would be most effective.' "

Piper gasped. "Prue was interested in Elena's tarot deck. She said it was really old. It couldn't be the same deck, could it?"

"I don't know," Phoebe answered. "But I understand now why Elena went pale when she drew that card. She knew it was a bad omen, connected to evil. I wonder if Elena knows the full story of Lascaris."

Piper rubbed her forehead. "I guess that's one of the things I'm going to try to find out tomorrow." She took another glance at the illustration. "Just looking at his picture gives me the creeps," she admitted.

Phoebe continued to read. " 'As Lascaris became more powerful, the women became weaker, and the men they kissed hovered near death. When the women were no longer strong enough to serve his needs, Lascaris would perform a ritual. When the ritual was complete, the men and women died.' "

Piper swallowed hard. "Nice guy."

"It says that Lascaris's spirit was imprisoned," Phoebe went on.

"Where?" Piper asked.

Phoebe shook her head, frustrated that the most important information had been left out. "It doesn't say where or by whom."

"Hold on a minute, Phoebe. If this warlock was imprisoned, then he isn't the one hurting Prue," Piper pointed out.

"I don't know," Phoebe disagreed. "Prue is kissing any and every guy who comes within

reach of her lips. It just sounds too . . . connected."
Then a horrifying thought hit her. "What if Lascaris escaped somehow and he's using Prue to strengthen his powers?"

Piper stared at her, terrified.

A sense of dread streamed through Phoebe's body. "We have to find him," she said, "We have to find him before he does the same thing to Prue that he did to all his other victims."

CHAPTER
11

Prue leaned against Lloyd Claiborne's wrought-iron balcony and gazed out at the bay.

Why do so many of my dreams take place here? she wondered. Is Claiborne somehow connected to that magical New Year's Eve kiss? Is he the one I've been searching for?

All around her, everything was shrouded in a gray mist. A thick fog rolled in, and soon she could no longer see the bay or the Golden Gate Bridge.

But she felt *his* presence.

The midnight phantom stood behind Prue, hovering, waiting. Breathing became difficult, and her body felt as though it had been ignited with invisible flames that burned but did not consume.

She wanted him, and at the same time she was

terrified of him. Fear and desire wound through her until she could no longer tell them apart.

She felt a pulsing just below her throat, a throbbing. She placed her hand over the emerald necklace that rested there, and she spun around.

The stranger stood before her, shrouded by shadows.

"You gave me life," he rasped, and placed his hands on either side of Prue's face. Weakness engulfed her. Her legs trembled so badly, she could barely stand upright. She couldn't move. She couldn't fight.

His mouth covered hers.

But this time the kiss was different. No passion. No desire.

Now there was nothing but the ugliness of the truth. He was cutting off her breath, draining her life. Everything closed in on her, suffocating her. . . .

Prue jerked awake. She felt her scream vibrate through the room.

But she couldn't hear it. She screamed again, but all she heard was the rapid thumping of her own heart.

She bolted upright in bed, breathing heavily, her body trembling. A cold sweat made her nightgown cling to her skin.

Something is wrong, she thought. Something is terribly wrong.

She couldn't feel the softness of the cotton sheets on her legs. She couldn't feel the weight of the quilt on her body or the bandage that Piper had taped around her hand.

Her peripheral vision was gone. It was as though she were staring down a tunnel. At the end was a light, but it was becoming smaller and smaller.

Gasping for breath and terrified, Prue tried to climb out of bed, but her body wouldn't cooperate. She fell on her side, no longer able to keep herself upright.

What's happening to me? her mind screamed.

Piper glanced around the Railyard Café, looking for the tarot reader. She was beginning to think Phoebe was right. Elena was behind whatever was happening to Prue. This whole mess started just after they had their fortunes told.

She walked up to the bar, where a man was stacking glasses. "Is the manager here?" she asked.

He turned and smiled at her. "That's me. What can I do for you?"

She twisted her hands together, wondering how to explain without saying too much. "Do you know where I can find Elena?"

He jerked his thumb over his shoulder. "In the back, giving a private reading."

Piper grimaced and glanced at her watch. "Thanks."

She walked around the bar toward the kitchen and the back room. She stopped in the doorway.

She saw Elena laying out her cards for a man with gleaming black hair. Piper saw only the back of his head, but something about him was familiar.

Maybe he's a customer at Quake, she thought.

Elena glanced at the doorway and gasped.

The man turned.

Robert!

Piper's breath caught. How do they know each other? she wondered. Have they been working together?

Piper stepped toward the table, determined to find out. "Well, now, isn't this an interesting coincidence," she began.

Elena's eyes widened. "You!" she cried, and quickly gathered up her cards.

"Wait a minute!" Piper said. "I just want to talk to you."

But Elena bolted out of the chair, grabbed it, and threw it in Piper's direction. Then she tore through the back door.

Piper leapt back, the chair missing her by inches. Giving Robert a fleeting glance, Piper jumped over the chair and raced after the fortune-teller.

She rushed outside and spotted Elena inside a green car. Instinctively Piper thrust out her hands and stopped time. She ran to the car and tried to open the door.

It was locked!

She swore under her breath. If only she'd gotten outside before Elena had locked the door.

Time unfroze.

Elena turned the ignition and barreled down the alley.

Piper felt her frustration mount. She'd just

blown their best chance to find out what was happening to Prue.

Then she remembered Robert. If she couldn't get answers from Elena, she'd get answers from him.

She ran back into the restaurant, but the table in the back room was empty.

Robert was gone.

Phoebe stood at the kitchen counter, holding Piper's cell phone in her hand. She couldn't believe her sister had forgotten to take it with her. Piper had promised to call Phoebe as soon as she knew something. And Phoebe couldn't stand it anymore—not knowing was driving her crazy!

Who is Lascaris? Where is he now? The questions kept running through her mind. Okay, Phoebe thought as she began to pace back and forth. What are the facts? He's a warlock from the 1700s. He's obsessed with a weird deck of tarot cards. He's got black hair and piercing blue eyes. He's French—

Phoebe gasped. A horrible thought occurred to her. What if Robert was Lascaris?

In some strange way it made sense. Maybe the problems didn't start after the tarot reading. Maybe they really began before—when Robert stopped by the table. He'd kissed Prue's hand.

A kiss was the key to Lascaris's power.

Granted, it wasn't much, but it was all Phoebe had to go on.

She stopped pacing. She was driving herself insane, running the different scenarios through her head. Robert, Lascaris, Elena, Prue.

How was it all related? Somehow they'd all become tangled, but Phoebe didn't know how or what she should do to unweave the fabric of magic that had such a strong hold on her sister.

She shook the cell phone in her hand. "Piper, why didn't you take your phone? I need to know what you've found out so I'll know what to do."

Frustrated, she headed up the stairs to Prue's room. She quietly opened the door and slipped inside.

Prue was lying in her bed, asleep. Phoebe couldn't believe how pale her sister had become.

An icy fear wound itself around Phoebe's heart. She felt incredibly helpless, undeniably useless. What good is my power to see the future if I can't help someone I love? she asked herself.

Out of the corner of her eye, something caught her attention. A slip of paper beside the phone on the bedside table. She picked it up. Piper had written a message for Prue to call Robert. Phoebe studied his phone number.

Without thinking, she picked up Prue's phone on the bedside table and dialed the number. It rang, and rang. No one was home. Phoebe sighed and hung up, almost relieved. What would I have said anyway. "Hi, Robert. This is Phoebe. I was wondering if you happened to be a two- or three-hundred-year-old warlock?"

She set down the message and spotted Prue's invitation to Lloyd Claiborne's New Year's Eve party. She ran her finger over the engraved lettering.

Lloyd Claiborne's party, she thought. Elena, Robert, and Prue were all there. Does Claiborne's mansion hold any of the answers?

Phoebe wasn't sure, but she *did* know that she couldn't wait there any longer. She had to do something for Prue. She glanced back at her sister. Prue was sleeping peacefully. She'll be all right, Phoebe thought.

I have to go to Claiborne's, Phoebe decided. I don't know what I'll find there, but maybe, with some luck and a little concentration, I can force a vision.

It wasn't much of a plan. Actually it was practically no plan at all. But at the moment it was all she had to go on.

Piper glanced around the bar area of Giovanni's. People in expensive clothes sat at small cocktail tables set with elegant candles. They sipped drinks from crystal glasses. No wonder Claiborne used this place to cater his New Year's Eve party, she thought. It's completely chic.

A waiter scurried by her, headed for the kitchen. She hurried after him. "Excuse me."

He stopped and looked at her. "Can I help you?"

"Did you serve food at Lloyd Claiborne's New Year's Eve party?" she asked.

"No, thank goodness."

"Why do you say that?" she asked.

"Because all the waiters who did got sick. Except for John over there." He pointed toward a man in a tuxedo, taking an order in a far corner.

"Thanks," Piper said, grateful to find someone who had been at the party. She waited impatiently while John finished taking the order. She stopped him on his way to the kitchen. "Excuse me, but I heard you worked the Claiborne party."

He looked uncomfortable as he shifted his stance. "Is this about all those guys getting sick?" he asked.

Piper nodded. "I'm interested in the guests. Do you remember anything about anyone?"

The waiter shook his head. "There were a lot of people there."

"Did you notice anyone unusual?" she asked, not wanting to give him the specifics of what she was looking for. It wouldn't do her any good to influence his answer.

He furrowed his brow. "Well, there was that lady dressed in black scarves. She gave a few people some tarot readings. Then there was that chick in red."

Piper heard the alarms going off in her mind. Prue had mentioned that everyone had worn black but her. She was definitely the one wearing red, but why would that make her unusual? "Why do you remember the one who wore red?"

The waiter shrugged. "After midnight she was kissing everyone in sight—everybody except me. Of course, now I'm glad that she didn't."

Piper narrowed her eyes. "Why are you glad?"

"Because I'm the only waiter at the party who

didn't get sick." He laughed. "All the other guys are in the hospital." He gave her a wink. "Maybe she carried some contagious disease. You know, like Typhoid Mary—she could be the one who made all the guys at Claiborne's get sick."

He thinks he's making a joke, Piper thought, stunned. But he may have found the connection. If Prue kissed the waiters and they got sick . . . she kissed Billy and he got sick . . . Piper's heart was racing. And the delivery guy. I saw him at the hospital after he kissed Prue.

Lascaris!

It's true. He's escaped somehow and put Prue under his spell. He's using the exact same evil he used centuries ago! Piper felt her fear rocket inside her. "Thanks," she told the waiter. "I really appreciate the information."

"Sure," the waiter replied, and went into the kitchen.

As soon as he was out of sight, Piper ran for the door. A few blocks from the restaurant, she riffled through her purse, searching for her cell phone. With a groan, she remembered exactly where it was—sitting at home on the kitchen counter. "Dumb, dumb, dumb," she said under her breath. She searched through her bag again. She didn't even have change for a pay phone.

She had to get back home to tell Phoebe. She started to walk out of the restaurant, when another thought stopped her in her tracks. Jake! They had a date at the Presidio today. Piper glanced at her watch and moaned. She couldn't even call him to cancel. He was probably already at the park!

I can't stand him up a second time, she decided. In a panic, Piper rushed to the Presidio. She got out of her car, her heart pounding. How would she explain to Jake—

And then she saw him, sitting on a quilt beneath a large tree. He was reaching into a wicker basket and setting out a picnic lunch.

Piper's heart tightened. She couldn't believe he'd gone to so much trouble after all the mishaps.

He saw her, grinned brightly, and got to his feet. "Piper," he called out happily.

"Oh, Jake," she said, knowing she would have to tell him that she couldn't stay. She crossed the grassy lawn, her chest feeling as though someone were wrapping a tight band around it. She didn't want to hurt Jake, but she knew she couldn't explain everything to him. Their relationship hadn't even begun really. It was too soon to reveal her most sacred secret.

"Hey, beautiful," he said as she neared.

Beautiful. He said it with such sincerity that she felt herself falling deeper. Piper wished she didn't have to leave him again, but she had to get back to Halliwell Manor. She had to tell Phoebe that Prue was definitely under Lascaris's charm. But how did it happen? When did Lascaris take control of Prue?

The toe of her shoe caught on a rock. With a startled screech, Piper lost her balance, and suddenly she was falling. All she saw was a pan of blueberry pie, and her face headed straight for it.

Strong arms grabbed her just in time, pulling her upright. Then she was standing, toe to toe with Jake, staring at his chest, mortified.

He tucked his finger beneath her chin, lifted her gaze to his, and grinned. "I knew you'd fall for me."

She gave an embarrassed laugh. "You know, a tarot reader told me that I was going to get noticed this year, but I didn't think it would turn out like this."

Jake pulled her close. "Well, you sure have my attention."

He lowered his head slightly.

He's going to kiss me, Piper realized. And I want him to. She tilted her head, waiting for his mouth to cover hers. I've never wanted someone to kiss me so much in my life. . . .

Then Piper suddenly pulled away—right before Jake kissed her. She realized something. Something very important. "I can't stay," she blurted out.

Jake jerked his head back as though she'd slapped him. "What? Why?"

"I have to . . . to do something."

He released his hold on her. "Go see Billy?"

"No. It's not that." She saw the disappointment in his eyes and desperately wished she could tell him more. "I'm really sorry. I can't explain—"

"Don't worry about it. I'll just pretend that I was creating a set for a movie where the hero and heroine have a picnic. And she runs out on him," he said sarcastically.

Piper knew that she had hurt him again. I'll make everything right between us later, she promised herself. "I'm really sorry," she repeated, and hurried to her car. She had to get home to Phoebe and Prue.

Why didn't I figure this out before? she wondered. Whatever is killing Prue began with that midnight kiss on New Year's Eve!

CHAPTER
12

Through a narrowing tunnel of vision, Prue watched the late-afternoon shadows creep into her room. She fought back tears, trying not to give in to complete terror.

Neither Phoebe nor Piper had checked on her in a while. She was afraid they were both gone, that she was alone in the house. She was terrified that no one knew she was slowly, agonizingly, dying.

She felt no pain, only the life being drawn from her.

She tried to sit up, but her muscles wouldn't respond. She couldn't roll to her side. She could only lie in her bed as she would soon lie in a coffin.

Unable to move, unable to feel the softness of her surroundings, unable to let anyone know that they shouldn't close the lid.

She felt a weightlessness, as though nothing existed except her spirit, as though her body had given up the struggle and had already surrendered to the inevitable.

She tried to scream, to speak, to moan, but if she was successful in any of her attempts, she was unaware of it. Her ears heard nothing, nothing but the silence.

She couldn't smell the potpourri she kept in the ceramic bowl on her dresser. She couldn't smell the lemon scent that always came with the sheets because Phoebe liked to use lemon-scented detergent when she did the laundry.

The tunnel was closing, her vision growing narrower and narrower. She didn't dare close her eyes for fear that when she opened them again, she would see only what she saw when they were closed—darkness.

She focused on the sunlight streaming through the window. She saw fewer and fewer rays, not because the sunlight was fading, but because the opening to the tunnel was growing smaller.

The world of everyday reality was fading away, and she was frighteningly aware that Elena's prediction was coming true. How much longer? she wondered. How much longer will it be before I'm totally surrounded by darkness?

"I don't usually allow unscheduled visitors into my home," Lloyd Claiborne said as Phoebe stepped into his grand foyer.

Her breath caught at its magnificence. No wonder Prue had wanted to come to his party. She must have felt as though she were in paradise, surrounded by all the antique furniture and artwork.

Phoebe balled her hands into fists. Come on, vision, she thought. Come to me. Prue was here. Tell me what I need to know.

She turned to Claiborne. "I'm sorry that I stopped by unannounced, but Prue is sick, and I have a few questions about your New Year's Eve party."

He sighed deeply. "Everyone has questions about it. I'm beginning to regret that I ever hosted that party. And, of course, I hope that Prue will get better quickly. What would you like to know?"

"Do you remember a guest named Elena?" she asked, wanting to get to the heart of the matter as quickly as possible.

He pursed his lips, then shook his head. "I don't know that name. If she was here, she must have come with one of my guests."

"What about Robert Galliard?"

"Ah, Robert, yes, I know him well."

She saw respect reflected in Claiborne's eyes, and she realized that she'd have to be discreet to avoid causing suspicion. Was Claiborne working with Robert?

"I met Robert just a little while ago," Phoebe confessed. "Prue told me he was an antiques dealer."

"One of the finest," Claiborne assured her.

"I've been doing business with Robert for the last ten years. Come into the library and I'll show you the chess set I bought from him—crystal and topaz, it's quite extraordinary."

I don't want to see a chess set, Phoebe thought. I want to find out what happened at your party.

But on the chance that the chess set might tell her something about Robert, she followed Claiborne up a grand staircase to the mezzanine.

Through the open door to her left, Phoebe could see book-lined walls. She passed a glass case, and her gaze fell on the three glittering necklaces it displayed.

Phoebe's breath caught, and she stopped walking. She saw a beautiful necklace, a gleaming emerald surrounded by gold. She placed both hands on the glass case and squeezed her eyes shut.

Vision, come to me, she ordered silently. She held tightly on to the case. I need a vision, she thought desperately. See something, Phoebe, see something! her mind shouted.

Phoebe furrowed her brow as she concentrated on calling up images that would help Prue. She felt her muscles grow tense, and pain bounced between her temples.

"Are you all right?" Claiborne asked.

Phoebe jerked her eyes open and looked at him. "I . . . uh . . . I was just admiring the jewelry."

He smiled. "With your eyes *closed?*"

She took a deep breath and rubbed her temples. I'll have this headache for the rest of the day. "I was imagining how they might look on me," she improvised.

"Very beautiful, I'm sure," he answered. "You asked about Robert before. Actually he's buying that emerald necklace for his shop in France."

"Do you know anything about its history?" Phoebe asked, searching for any clue that might help her.

He shrugged. "It came from France, and it's at least three hundred years old. That's really all I know aside from the cut and weight of the stone."

France? Phoebe repeated to herself. Like Lascaris and Robert.

"But here, let me show you the chess set," Claiborne said, and led her into the library.

Although Phoebe's headache intensified, she tried to focus on the chess set. She even moved a crystal knight and a topaz queen across the jeweled board. But apart from the fact that the chess set was beautiful, she didn't pick up anything from it. No visions, no vibes. Nothing about Robert. She shook her head, pressing her fingers against her temples. "I'm sorry," she told Lloyd Claiborne. "I've got a splitting headache. I've got to go. Thank you for your help."

She left the room, again passing the glass case. Her head throbbing with pain. Then a bright light flashed into Phoebe's eyes. Electricity jolted her. I did it! she realized. It's a vision! Phoebe closed her eyes—and images began to appear in her mind:

*   *   *

Prue entwined in a passionate embrace with a cloaked man.

A cloak decorated with the symbols of the black tower card.

They kiss.

He drops her to the floor in a lifeless heap.

The tower card from Elena's deck slowly floating down.

Landing on Prue's lips.

A final kiss of death . . .

Phoebe came out of her trance, shaken to the core.

The meaning of the vision wasn't completely clear. Only one thing was. *I have to get back to the house,* Phoebe realized. *Prue doesn't have much time left!*

CHAPTER 13

Phoebe stood beside Prue's bed, her heart aching at the sight of her sister. Prue stared back at her from eyes sunk deep in their sockets.

She saw Prue's lips barely moving. She bent down so that her ear touched Prue's mouth.

"Darkness," Prue rasped.

"You're not talking about the night, are you?" Phoebe asked, her eyes burning with tears. "You're being surrounded by darkness."

Prue closed her eyes as though relieved that Phoebe had understood her.

"Don't worry, Prue," Phoebe said in a voice filled with a confidence she didn't feel. "Piper and I know what's behind this, and we're going to find a way to stop it. So you just hold on."

She hurried out of the room and up the stairs to the attic. She rushed to *The Book of Shadows* and turned to the page that described Lascaris. She read the words again slowly, trying to determine if a message had been hidden within them.

The story appeared straightforward, but somewhere there had to be a clue. He had been imprisoned and somehow he had escaped.

But where was his prison? Who had put him there? And how had he managed to escape?

Okay, Phoebe thought. Let's try this from another angle. Who out of the men Prue kissed didn't get sick? A midnight phantom and Robert. Could they be one and the same? Or had the midnight phantom taken ill as well, and they just didn't know it because no one knew who he was?

Robert wasn't sick. That she *did* know.

Maybe Claiborne was Lascaris. It was his party. He made out the guest list. He invited Prue. But had he kissed her?

So many loose ends. So many whos, whats, whys, and ifs. How could she make sense of any of it?

Piper burst into the attic, and Phoebe nearly jumped out of her skin.

"I found the connection between the sick men at the two New Year's parties," Piper said breathlessly. "Prue kissed them all. So the spell—or whatever it is—had to start with the guy who gave Prue that midnight kiss."

Phoebe nodded in total agreement. "I went to Claiborne's, and I had a vision. I saw Lascaris kissing Prue. He was draining the life from her."

"Which means he's escaped," Piper concluded.

"Maybe he's got some connection with Claiborne or his house," Phoebe told her. "Maybe that's why I had a vision there."

"In your vision," Piper said eagerly, "did you see how he escaped?"

"No," Phoebe admitted. "And I don't know how to imprison—" She broke off and leapt back from *The Book of Shadows*. The pages of the book were quickly flipping themselves. "W-w-what's it doing?" she asked.

Piper rushed to the book. "There has to be a reason for this," she said. "It's trying to tell us something!"

Phoebe cautiously stepped closer to the podium again. Phoebe stared at the page the book had stopped on. It showed a necklace—a beautiful oval emerald set in a band of gold.

"This is giving me the willies," Phoebe said. "Claiborne showed me this necklace. He's selling it to Robert for his shop in France!"

Phoebe's heart raced as she read the words. "It says that the emerald necklace belonged to a witch who fought a very powerful warlock named Lascaris. The witch imprisoned Lascaris inside the emerald with a spell that gave the warlock only one chance to escape every century: at 12:01 A.M., New Year's Day.

Phoebe turned to Piper, her excitement building. "Okay, I know exactly what happened. Lascaris—better known to us as Robert—somehow escaped from the necklace at Claiborne's party!"

Piper shook her head. "That's not it, Phoebe.

We met Robert that afternoon *before* the party, which means that he's not Lascaris. And it's not Claiborne, because Prue said she'd been doing business with him for a long time."

"Then who is Lascaris?"

"Someone we don't know, someone we've never seen before midnight of New Year's Eve," Piper said with conviction.

Phoebe heard Prue moan loudly from her room—and a horrifying thought occurred to her. She whispered, "Maybe he's someone we can't see at all."

"What are you talking about?" Piper asked.

Phoebe grabbed Piper's shoulders. "I had my vision at Claiborne's while I was near the glass case that held the necklace. What if Prue was standing in that spot at midnight? Remember, she said the lights went out. She kissed someone, and when the lights came back on, no one was there."

Piper stared at her. "Are you saying what I think you are?"

"Lascaris's spirit escaped from the necklace at midnight and somehow got inside Prue through their kiss!"

Phoebe watched Piper begin to pace. "Okay, let's think rationally here."

"We're dealing with a warlock, Piper. There's nothing remotely rational about the situation," Phoebe pointed out. "Lascaris has been imprisoned in that emerald for who knows how long. He was probably weak when he escaped—too frail to regain the life force that he needs to survive outside it. So he forces Prue to kiss men, and through her kisses he steals their strength. Which is why nearly everyone she kissed got sick. But at the same time that Lascaris is getting stronger, Prue is getting weaker—because she's a conduit!"

Piper stopped pacing and blinked. "You couldn't have come up with a theory that's a little less complicated?"

Phoebe shrugged. "Sorry."

"Okay, it's complicated," Piper said. "So what do we do now?"

"We need to trap a warlock," Phoebe replied. "And we need to get that emerald necklace."

"Phoebe, you know we could go to jail for this," Piper whispered as she pressed Lloyd Claiborne's doorbell.

"Only if we're caught," Phoebe assured her, "and you're here to make sure that doesn't happen."

A butler opened the door, and with a wave of her hands, Piper froze time. The man's mouth was open. The breeze had lifted his toupee and held it just above his scalp.

"Lead the way," Piper ordered, "but be quick about it. I never know when this freeze stuff is going to wear off."

She followed Phoebe into the house, hurrying across the foyer and up the stairs to the second floor. The only sound was the echo of their shoes hitting the marble floor. Piper glanced around quickly, her nervousness increasing.

Phoebe stopped in front of a glass display case. "Oh, no," she moaned. "I don't believe it!"

"What? What's wrong?" Piper asked, dreading the answer.

Phoebe spun around. "It's gone! The necklace is gone."

"Great!" Piper whispered harshly. "Now what?"

"We hope that Robert hasn't already taken it, and that it's still here," Phoebe said.

"And where do you suggest we look?"

"Claiborne's library."

"Why there?"

"Because it's the only other room he showed me!"

Phoebe was sounding panicky now, and Piper decided to stop asking questions and just look for the necklace. She followed Phoebe to the library, passing a grandfather clock. No ticking, no sound. Even though her power had caused the silence, Piper always found it a little surprising.

In the library, behind Claiborne's massive desk, Phoebe was frantically opening drawers and shuffling through papers.

Piper approached cautiously—and noticed a large velvet box on the corner of the desk. She opened it and looked at the stunning emerald necklace. "Is this what we're looking for?" she asked.

Phoebe looked up, and released a sigh of relief. "He must be getting ready to sell it to Robert."

"Which means we don't have much time," Piper told her. "Let's get out of here."

Piper removed the necklace from the velvet case and clutched it in her hand. She placed the empty box on the corner of the desk—right where she'd found it. Then she raced out of the library and through the foyer, Phoebe close on her heels.

She felt giddy with relief as they ran out of the mansion and made it safely into her car. "We did it!" she cried.

"Now let's get back to Prue," Phoebe replied.

Time returned to normal as Piper drove her car back to Halliwell Manor. She pulled up in front of the house, and her heart nearly dropped to the floorboards. Jake was standing on the front porch.

"We've got company," Phoebe said.

"And he couldn't have picked a worse time," Piper added bleakly. She knew she had no choice but to tell him to leave. She had to put Prue first.

"You're going to have to get rid of him and fast," Phoebe said.

"No kidding," Piper replied, handing Phoebe the emerald necklace. She got out of the car and walked toward the house.

With a grin, Jake strolled toward her.

"Piper, we don't have a lot of time," Phoebe whispered. "I'll get things ready."

Piper watched her sister rush into the house.

Jake gazed at Phoebe with surprise. "What's her hurry? Where's the fire?"

"No fire," Piper told him. "We just . . . have some things we need to take care of."

"I guess this is a bad time to drop by unexpectedly?"

That's a gross understatement, Piper thought.

"I didn't like the way things ended at our picnic," Jake said quietly.

"Neither did I," Piper admitted.

He took her hand, and she felt warmth swirl through her. His gaze drifted to her eyes. "I like you, Piper. I want to get to know you."

"Me too, but—"

"If I'm wasting my time, please let me know."

"You're not. I like you, too." Piper replied. "A lot."

"Our dates always end before they really get started." He cradled her cheek with his palm and brushed his thumb over her lips, making them tingle. "All day, all night, I can't get you out of my mind. I can't stop wondering what it would be like to kiss you."

Piper swallowed hard.

"Would you mind if I kissed you now?" he asked.

A slow grin crossed Piper's face. Jake cupped her face between his hands and lowered his mouth to hers.

"Piper, I need you," Phoebe cried. "Now!"

Piper pulled back, feeling only the whisper of his lips touching hers. She glanced at the house. Phoebe was leaning out Prue's window on the second floor.

Piper looked back at Jake, hoping he'd understand and forgive her yet again. "I've got to go."

"Is there something wrong?" he asked. "Something I can do to help?"

Piper wished he *could* help in some way, but she knew the only answer was for him to leave. "There's nothing wrong. It's just a . . . a sister thing."

He moved his hands away from her face and stepped back. "Are you sure that's what it is?"

"Come on," Phoebe said. "It's important."

"Please, don't give up on me, Jake, but I have to go, and I don't have time to explain."

Her heart aching, she rushed into the house, leaving him standing alone on the front lawn.

She hurried up the stairs and into Prue's room. She stopped, heartsick at the sight of her older sister lying in bed. Prue's skin had lost all its vibrancy. Her flesh seemed to have withered from her bones. Dark blue circles surrounded her closed eyes. Her breathing was shallow and raspy, as though a hand had tightened around her throat.

"Let's get to *The Book of Shadows*," Phoebe said.

Piper nodded and followed Phoebe to the attic.

"A spell," Phoebe murmured as she placed the necklace on the stand beside the book. "We need the spell to send his spirit back into the emerald." She frantically flipped pages.

Phoebe stopped and released a deep sigh. "I found it. Listen to this. 'Ashes to ashes, dust to dust / We imprison you because we must / To spare the innocent, to protect the meek, We reduce your evil power to very weak / Into a prison you must go / Never again to be our foe.' "

Piper felt a rush of relief. "That sounds like it'll work. What do we need?"

"Ashes from a fire, spiderwebs, sage, mistletoe, and candles," Phoebe read.

"I can get ashes from the hearth in the living room," Piper said. "Candles are no problem, I've got sage in the kitchen, Piper said.

"I'll get the mistletoe and spiderwebs," Phoebe added, scanning the attic. "I'm sure I can find both of them around here."

"And then what?" Piper asked.

"I don't know," Phoebe replied. "The Power of Two?"

CHAPTER
14

With increasing dread, Prue watched her peripheral vision continue to shrink until she could see only a pinprick of light. A moment later the tiny spark disappeared.

Prue could no longer see the room around her. But one thing she saw clearly. Within her mind's eye, she saw the mysterious stranger. He was more real than ever.

He placed an icy hand on her forehead.

"It is time for you to know all," he said in a low voice. "You are mine now. I control you."

"But you said my kisses give you life," she reminded him.

He laughed. "Not when I kiss you, but when you kiss others. It is through you that I obtain the strength of young men. The strength that keeps me alive."

Now Prue understood. She was never obsessed with kissing—*he* was. She was feeling his need for energy—and she fed him. Every time she kissed a man she fed this monster!

"Robert," she said weakly.

He growled and moved away from her. "He was powerful. He could have given much to me, but you were too slow. You waited for his kiss. After that he was useless to me."

Her revulsion of Robert was *his* revulsion, Prue realized. With regret, she remembered the cruel things she had said to Robert. Would he ever forgive her?

Prue felt as though she were being crushed by her own shame. From the moment this phantom kissed her, he'd wormed his way through her mind, controlling her thoughts and actions, making them his own.

She realized with startling clarity that she no longer had the strength to serve him as he required. He would soon discard her. And worst of all, she now realized he was not the man of her dreams, but a parasitic spirit residing within her, feeding on her.

He was inside her, part of her, cutting off the true world that surrounded her, until her world narrowed down to only him.

For the first time, Prue noticed that he wore a bright red cloak—the color of fresh blood. In gold, the same odd designs that were part of the tower card decorated his cloak—symbols of power and destruction.

He floated behind a large golden altar and held out his hands to Prue, hands with long, slender fingers and talonlike nails.

Rings of red light circled each of his fingers as he raised his hands above his head. Fire leapt out from the rings.

He laughed, his eyes twinkling with evil, and Prue knew she was a pawn about to be sacrificed.

No, she thought, her senses failing. I won't go without a fight.

From beneath the cloak's hood, his eyes burned into her. She couldn't look away. He had the power to reach beyond the darkness—to be seen, to be felt, to be heard.

Everything was gone but his world. Only through him do I still feel alive, she realized with horror.

His power terrified her. And yet she knew she would make one last stand and face him with the only thing that remained truly hers: a faltering courage.

"Come here," he commanded.

His voice traveled through her, absorbing her, wrapping around her like a shroud.

I won't go, she thought. I won't allow this to happen.

But her legs moved. She walked toward him.

No! her mind screamed. I won't come to you. But she couldn't stop herself from obeying his command.

She couldn't stop herself from walking toward

the golden altar where he waited with triumph glowing in his eyes.

With Piper's help, Phoebe placed Prue on the old couch in the attic. Phoebe wasn't sure if Prue was even aware they had carried her out of her room.

It was as though her arms and legs, her whole body, had given up. Prue was unconscious yet she murmured incoherently.

The warlock had taken her far beyond their reach.

"I don't know if this spell will work," Piper said. "I don't even know why we brought her up here."

"We need the Power of Three to send this warlock's spirit back into the necklace," Phoebe said. "We can't do it alone."

Piper nodded. "What do I do first?"

"With the ashes, draw a large oval on the floor. Then we'll place Prue in its center."

Phoebe placed candles around the area where Piper was drawing the oval. When Piper finished her task, Phoebe smudged the area with sage.

"For purity," Phoebe said quickly.

Then she broke off the red mistletoe berries and placed them around the outer edge of the oval. "Lovers meet and kiss under mistletoe. Now it will restore the power he stole through his kisses."

In the center of the oval, she laid the spider-webs. "To capture our prey." She stepped out of the oval. "All right, let's move Prue to its center."

Struggling alongside Piper, Phoebe got Prue into the center of the oval. Whispering the incantation from *The Book of Shadows*, Phoebe went from candle to candle, lighting the wicks until a circle of flames surrounded Prue. Then Phoebe took the emerald necklace and placed it on Prue's chest, right above her faintly beating heart.

"What if this doesn't work?" Piper asked, her voice shaking.

"Don't even go there," Phoebe commanded. "We're running out of time. We may have only one chance. Come into the oval and kneel."

Looking at Prue's pale face, Phoebe felt the determination build within her. No warlock is going to take my sister from me, she vowed silently. She joined Piper inside the oval and knelt.

"Join hands," Phoebe ordered, grabbing one of Piper's hands and one of Prue's. "And remember. It's only a warlock's spirit. One witch imprisoned him before. This time he'll have three sending him back into the emerald. I'll chant the incantation first, then we'll repeat it together. If Prue is too weak to say it, she can think it."

Piper nodded and Phoebe gave her hand a quick squeeze for courage. She drew a deep breath to begin the chant.

Then the door to the attic burst open. Phoebe jerked her head around. Elena stood in the doorway, her scarves whipping around her.

Terrified, Phoebe released her hold of Prue and Piper and rose to her feet. "It's just like my vision," she cried. "She's here to kill Prue!"

CHAPTER
15

Elena!

How did she get in? Piper wondered, and what did she want?

Piper shadowed Phoebe's movements as she crossed the attic. Grabbing Elena's arms, they pushed her back against the wall, keeping her away from Prue.

"I'm here to help," Elena told them.

"Yeah, right," Piper said. "How did you get in here anyway?"

"I picked the lock on the front door."

Piper stared at her. "And you want us to trust you?"

"You don't understand," Elena said.

"I think we do," Phoebe told her.

What now? Piper thought with panic. We can't

let her go. And we certainly can't let her see our powers.

"Phoebe, can you hold her?" she asked.

Phoebe tightened her grip on the fortune-teller. "For now."

Piper rushed over to an old chest in the corner and grabbed several lengths of rope, which she brought back to Phoebe.

Phoebe forced Elena to turn around. Ignoring the woman's protests, Piper pulled her arms behind her back and secured her hands with the rope. Then she spun her back around.

"I can help," Elena insisted. "I *must* help. It is written in the cards."

"The only thing written in the cards is that you can't be trusted," Phoebe said.

"I swear to you that I'm here to help. You must believe me," Elena told them.

Piper studied her. "You want us to trust you? Tell me why you were reading Robert Galliard's cards."

Elena shrugged. "I met him at Lloyd Claiborne's party. He came to me to see if your sister would ever love him."

"You make it sound so innocent," Phoebe said.

"Because it was," Elena insisted.

"Then why did you run from me at the Railyard Café?" Piper demanded.

"Because I knew that something evil had fallen upon all of you! I—I didn't want to get involved," Elena confessed. "But then I did a reading of my own. The cards made it very clear that I had to find you and help you. But I don't know what I need to do."

To Piper the confession sounded like a con. "You need to stay out of our way."

She glanced over her shoulder as she heard Prue moan. Prue's chest was rising and falling as though it carried a great weight. Sweat beaded her sister's brow.

Piper looked at Phoebe. "We don't have time for this. We need to get her out of here."

"How about the hallway?" Phoebe suggested.

"No! You must let me help you!" Elena protested as they shoved her out of the room and into the stairwell.

Using another piece of rope, Piper secured her to the railing. The woman was still ranting as the two sisters returned to the attic. "Without me you can never succeed!" she cried. "I read it in the cards!"

She found Phoebe in the oval, kneeling over Prue. "Hurry up. We're losing her," Phoebe murmured. "Her pulse is weakening, and her breathing is way too shallow."

Piper knelt, took Prue's hand and then Phoebe's.

Phoebe took a deep breath and began the incantation.

"I call on the Power of Three.
Ashes to ashes, dust to dust,
We imprison Lascaris because we must.
To spare the innocent, to protect the meek,

We reduce your evil power to very weak.
Into the prison you must go,
Never again to be our foe."

Piper closed her eyes and repeated the incantation with Phoebe once, twice, three times. The final time, she felt a glimmer of energy sweep through her. She opened her eyes.

Prue appeared unchanged. Her breathing was erratic, her face ashen.

Piper felt sick with dread. The spell failed, she realized. Prue is dying. She stared at Phoebe, who was stroking Prue's face and blinking back tears. "What did we do wrong?" Piper asked her

"We didn't do anything wrong," Phoebe answered. "Prue is too weak to complete the link. Without the full Power of Three, we have no hope of saving her."

CHAPTER 16

Phoebe couldn't believe it. Lascaris's darkness had overpowered them. Prue was fading with each passing moment, fading into a place where they would never be able to reach her—a place far beyond the realm of their magic powers.

"There has to be a spell that's strong enough to work with just the two of us," she said. She pounded her fist on *The Book of Shadows*. "One powerful, evil warlock needs to be banished back to his prison, and we don't know how to do it . . . unless . . ." She thought of her vision. "Elena must know something."

Piper raised her head. "You trust her?"

"No," Phoebe answered. "But right now she's all we've got."

Piper jerked open the door to the attic. Phoebe followed her into the stairwell. Elena glanced up, and Phoebe was surprised to see that her eyes were filled with fear. The woman definitely knew something.

Piper crouched in front of Elena. "Tell us about the tarot card, the one that predicted she'd be surrounded by darkness."

Elena darted her glance at Phoebe before turning her attention back to Piper. "I know only that it is the most powerful card in the deck—and the most deadly. My family believes that the cards choose you. When I do a reading, the right card places itself in my hand. So we've always been grateful that the tower card almost never shows up in a reading. I've never drawn it before—not until I placed it in front of your sister."

Her voice held such sincerity that Phoebe was having a hard time not believing her.

"And the tarot cards told you to come here?" she asked.

Elena nodded reluctantly. "I know only that you need my help to save your sister. I was hoping you would know what I'm supposed to do."

"Well, we don't!" Piper snapped. She got to her feet and glared at Elena. "We don't know, and our sister is dying!"

Phoebe slowly stood up, her earlier vision filling her mind.

"Wait a minute. Maybe we do know." She turned to Piper and took her arm. "When I had the vision of Elena standing over Prue, I thought she there to hurt her. Maybe I was wrong. Maybe she was helping us save her."

Piper's eyes slid to the fortune-teller. "And if you're wrong? If she's an instrument of Lascaris's?"

"Who is Lascaris?" Elena asked.

"A warlock who used the tarot cards to choose his victims," Phoebe said as she untied the ropes that bound Elena. She knew that if the tarot reader was to be effective in helping them, she needed to know everything. "He's taken possession of our sister's body and is using her to regain his strength and powers."

Piper grabbed Elena's chin and forced her to look at her. "And we're witches, but we won't harm you—as long as you're being straight with us."

"I—I swear it," Elena said.

Phoebe knelt in front of the tarot reader. It's my turn to make this woman squirm before we trust her with Prue's life, she thought.

"We have to get the spirit of Lascaris out of Prue and back into an eternal prison. If you are lying to us, I promise that I'll put *you* in the prison with him."

"I'm not lying," Elena insisted.

Phoebe nodded. "Okay. We'll do the spell again—only this time Elena will stand in the middle of the oval, holding the tower card over Prue, just as she did in my vision."

Prue heard a roaring, like the ocean churned up during a storm. Sound. Beautiful sound.

Then it began to fade, and she wanted to weep at its loss.

Gradually the roaring disappeared, but her ability to hear remained, and she heard the sweetest sounds: her sisters' voices united in a chant. She listened closely. There was another voice chanting with them—a voice she didn't recognize.

But it didn't matter. She knew that they'd figured out what was happening to her, that they were trying to fight the stranger who possessed her.

She had to help them. She knew they would need the strength of the Power of Three.

The cloaked man set two black candles on either end of his altar. On the table was a piece of parchment. Squinting, Prue read the words.

"Evil you are, evil you shall remain, but not in this world where you inflict pain/The kiss you gave others took their life/The kiss I gave you sliced our bond like a knife/My lips to yours is the stronger power/Within the emerald, live inside your blackened tower."

Were those his words—or the words that could defeat him? She shuddered. The words were written in blood.

She stared at him, summoning her powers of telekinesis, determined to blast him into oblivion—but nothing happened.

She was too weak. He'd drained her powers just as he was draining the life from her. How was she going to help her sisters defeat this monster without her power?

She thought about the words on the parchment. A kiss had given him life; another would slice their bond like a knife.

Then she realized what she had to do.

She felt her sisters' strength streaming into her.

If she could hear them, then maybe, just maybe, her other senses would return, her other abilities. She tried to form the words, to repeat the chant.

It was barely a whisper, but she felt the chant vibrating deep within her throat. "The Power of Three . . . spare innocent . . . until it is weak . . . never again to be our foe."

Within her mind, Lascaris had created another world, a world where his power grew as he stole life from others. A world he would destroy with his next sacrifice—her.

She knew that once he killed her, he would no longer be confined to the world of shadows. Her death would set him free in the everyday world, with no need for a conduit to destroy his future victims.

Which meant that in this world, enclosed by the darkness that she now shared with this man, she had to stop him.

She watched as he took the parchment from the altar. "And now a test," he said mockingly. He touched the edge of the parchment to the flame of a candle, and she watched it curl into ashes.

He brushed the soot from his fingers. "My powers are nearly at full strength again," he said, sounding pleased. "I couldn't destroy that until they were. You have been an enormous help to me. And now," he went on, his voice tinged with mock sorrow, "it is time for us to say farewell. Come to me and give me eternal life."

Prue's heart thundered within her chest. She didn't want to obey, didn't want to go anywhere near him, yet she knew she had no choice.

She felt herself walking through the darkness, toward the altar. As she neared, dark blood rose from the floor like a fountain on either side of the altar.

She stepped closer to him.

"Yes, Prue," he rasped. "I have called you here for the final sacrifice."

He pulled back the hood of his cloak that had always kept his face hidden.

Her midnight phantom.

He was handsome beyond belief, just as Prue had always imagined him. A man any woman would desire—and fall victim to.

But the handsome surface was a mask for putrefied evil, and Prue saw through it now, saw him for what he truly was. Ugly, blackened flesh hung off his face. His rancid odor assailed her nostrils. Hatred and triumph swirled in his eyes.

Prue cringed as he placed his hands on either side of her face. "Thank you, Prue," he told her. "Thank you for giving me back my life."

Always before, he had kissed her, taken her mouth, her strength, and her power. This time, Prue knew it was *she* who had to take from *him*.

Prue felt everything in her recoil at the thought,

but she lunged forward anyway, pressing her lips against his for a final, repulsive kiss.

Piper felt energy surge through her, crackling through the attic.

On the floor, in the center of the oval Prue writhed. Were they helping her—or making her worse?

The emerald necklace resting on Prue's chest began to glow and pulse as though it was suddenly a living thing.

Piper felt Phoebe's hand tighten on hers as they held each other and Prue. Elena stood over them, holding the tower card. She was white with fear, trembling, but Piper could feel that she, too, was pouring all her energy into fighting the evil that was destroying Prue.

Then a blinding flash of light filled the room. Prue's body convulsed.

She's dying, Piper thought. She's dying and we can't save her! She watched in horror as blood seeped from every pore of Prue's body. Piper felt something inside her breaking. We've lost her! And yet she continued the chant, not daring to stop.

Then a flickering form began to emerge. Slowly passing through her sister as though she were only a shadow.

Lascaris.

He was both the most beautiful and the most chilling being Piper had ever seen. She stammered, almost losing the chant, but she forced herself to concentrate on the spell.

She released Phoebe's hand, lifted up the necklace, and held it high over her head, directing it at the creature who had been living inside her sister.

A new and terrible fear swept through her as the warlock shifted into his true form—rotting flesh, blackened teeth, cold eyes, blood trickling from his mouth. He hovered over a listless Prue, and Piper knew that he was still feeding on her, draining the last of her life.

"Into a prison you must go!" Piper cried.

Lascaris turned to Piper, capturing and holding her gaze. His laugh echoed through the attic. "You are too late," he told her. "I am strong. I am free!"

CHAPTER 17

Prue felt an unforgiving pain sweep through her.

She'd kissed him. She'd forced herself to suffer the stench of his rotting skin, the touch of his decaying lips.

But her kiss hadn't destroyed him. It had simply freed him from the world he'd created.

Prue felt a stirring inside her—and she realized something else had happened during that hellish kiss. It had given her a power over him that no one else had, but he didn't know it.

Her thoughts were her own, no longer controlled by him. Her body was again hers completely, absolutely.

He was gone. The evil that had resided in her was now free.

Free to find his own victims.

She couldn't allow it. She *wouldn't*.

Now she had to regain what was hers by right and by sacrifice. Slowly, steadily, Prue fought back the darkness. She saw a tiny prick of light. Gradually the light grew, the dark shadows melting into it, disappearing as though they'd never been there.

The circle of light widened and began to fan out, and Prue realized that her peripheral vision was back. The darkness was gone. She felt the life surge back into her body. In the blink of a moment, all her other senses awakened. She felt the wood of the attic floor beneath her. She felt heat from the flames of a dozen candles flickering nearby.

Her senses had returned, but her mind was still sluggish.

And then she saw *him*.

"His name is Lascaris," she heard Phoebe say as if from a great distance. "He's a warlock."

I know, Prue wanted to tell her sister, but she was too weak.

She saw him clearly now—in his true grotesque form, hovering over her. His decayed flesh and teeth. Eyes in which evil swirled. Eyes that delighted in horror and destruction.

"I am free," he said. A wide grin exposed his greenish black teeth.

Not for long, Prue vowed, remembering the words on the parchment.

Lascaris turned to Piper, and Prue felt her heart constrict. "No," she said weakly.

Lascaris smiled and crooked a finger. "I need

more life." He moved slowly toward Piper. "Take my kiss and rejoice that I bestowed it upon you."

Prue saw Piper wave her arms as though to stop time.

Lascaris's laughter bounced off the walls and shook the ceiling. "Your insignificant power cannot stop me!"

Prue saw the panic fill Piper's eyes as he came nearer. Her power was useless against him.

Piper knelt and grabbed Prue's arm, trying to get her to sit up. "Prue, we need the Power of Three, and we need it now."

She felt Phoebe's arm around her, helping her to sit. If only she could stand, Prue thought.

Lascaris approached, and Prue tried to use her power to hold him at bay.

But she was still too weak. Too weak to stand. Too weak to use her powers. But not too weak to speak.

Prue struggled to her knees. She felt Piper and Phoebe laboring to help her. She didn't know if she could banish him. But I have to try, she thought.

Prue wanted to tell her sisters to run, to save themselves, but she knew without them she had no hope of winning.

The Power of Three.

She felt Elena's arm come around her waist, and then she was standing.

Fire flashed from the rings on Lascaris's fingers but failed to ignite anything.

"I'm impressed," he rasped. "Perhaps I shall take one more kiss from you after all."

Prue slowly shook her head. "I don't think so. Evil you are, evil you shall remain, but not in this world, where you can inflict pain."

She gasped for breath, her legs trembling. "The kiss you gave others took their life / The kiss I gave you sliced our bond like a knife / My lips to yours is the stronger power / Within the emerald, live inside your blackened tower."

Lascaris's evil laugh echoed around the room again. "Do you think you have power over *me*?"

Prue felt her sisters' arms around her more solidly, giving her more strength.

In a steady voice, she repeated the words, her sisters joining in the chant. She felt her strength growing. She began the chant again and heard Elena's voice join in.

And then she saw what Elena was holding. The tarot card with the symbols that matched Lascaris's robe.

The black tower.

She jerked the card away from Elena, knowing that she, Prue, was the center of the world he'd created. In taking everything from her, he'd given her the sole power to destroy him. And when she chose to kiss him, she accepted that responsibility.

She held the card before her and chanted again.

"No!" Lascaris cried out when he saw the card. "Not again!" He writhed in pain. "You are fools if you think you can return me to the prison."

But as they chanted, the Power of Three was building, binding him, twisting him in its relentless grip. "No!" he cried. "Don't send me back! I can give you powers beyond your wildest dreams! You can become my brides. All of you! And we shall rule the world!"

"I've seen your world," Prue told him. "Lived in it. I don't like it."

Tightening her hold on the card, she repeated the chant again.

Lascaris bellowed as a blinding green light shot out from the necklace Piper held in her hand. It wrapped around him like a shroud, covering him completely.

"No!" he screamed

His body bucked and jerked.

Prue felt her strength growing, power surging through her. She grabbed the emerald necklace from Piper and tossed it into the oval on the floor. Using her powers, she shoved Lascaris back until he stood over the magnificent jewel, completely imprisoned within the green light.

She repeated the chant one final time.

The fiery green glow pulled in Lascaris's writhing form—and he disappeared into the emerald.

CHAPTER
18

Piper hurried toward the Railyard Café, where she was supposed to meet her sisters for lunch. It had been a week since they'd banished Lascaris's spirit back into the emerald necklace.

It's amazing what a little spell will do, she thought happily. Everyone who'd gotten sick from Prue's kiss had recovered. Billy was back at work, creating new and wonderful appetizers. Everything was back to normal.

She rushed up the steps, missed one, and with a tiny groan, stumbled. Before her knees hit the ground, she felt strong arms catch and steady her. She lifted her gaze and stared into Jake's smiling brown eyes. Her breath caught. "What are you doing here?"

"Research."

She straightened and stepped out of his embrace. She hadn't seen or heard from him since she left him out on her front lawn. She'd given up hope of ever seeing Jake again.

"Research?" she asked.

He nodded with a grin. "Yeah. Do you have a minute?"

She pointed at the door to the café. "I'm supposed to meet my sisters—" She stopped. What am I doing? There isn't any evil lurking at the moment. For once this is not an emergency. "Sure. I have several minutes, in fact."

"Great. I need your opinion on something."

He took her hand. She loved the feel of his hand around hers. He led her to the side of the restaurant, where a red caboose was set up for outside dining. He guided her up the metal steps and inside. Piper looked around in surprise. There were tables set up but no customers.

He backed into a corner, wedging himself between the back wall of the caboose and a table. He pulled her closer to him.

Her heart hammered hard against her ribs, and she felt a tiny tremble rush through her. She smelled his cologne and saw the tiny smile lines around his eyes.

"I'm designing sets for a new movie. The hero has been having a hard time getting the heroine alone so he can . . . kiss her. He wants to take her to dinner, someplace unusual. Maybe someplace like this."

"Alone? Here? This place is usually packed with people," she explained.

"I thought the hero would make arrangements with the manager so that no other customers were allowed inside. It would be just the two of them and candlelight. Do you think the heroine would find it romantic?"

Piper smiled. "I think she would find it insanely romantic."

"Do you think she would mind if the hero kissed her before they met for dinner?"

Swallowing hard, Piper looked into the depths of his eyes. She saw doubt flicker for a heartbeat, but more than that, she saw genuine interest. "I know she wouldn't mind at all."

A grin crept across his face. "Good."

He lowered his mouth to hers. Piper closed her eyes, rose up on her toes, and wrapped her arms around his neck.

The kiss was even more than she'd anticipated. Filled with warmth and tenderness, it made her feel special, as though she were the only woman he'd ever cared about. When it ended, she felt breathless, light-headed, and completely happy.

She looked up at him, his arms around her.

"I'll pick you up at seven tonight," he said quietly.

"I'll be ready. I promise no excuses, no interruptions, and no disappearing acts."

He moved his arms from around her and took her hand. "Do you think the heroine would like it if the hero ended the date with another kiss?"

"Definitely," she said grinning. "A nice, long kiss."

He nodded. "I don't have much say in what goes into the script. I just design sets, but I'll see if we can work in a kiss at the end of the date."

Piper took a small step toward him. "Actually the heroine wouldn't mind if you ended your research with another kiss."

"Seems fair enough after I had to wait so long to get the first one," he said just before he covered her mouth with his.

"What is that secret smile that you've been wearing ever since you walked in here?" Phoebe asked Piper.

Piper's grin grew. "I *fell* into Jake's arms—literally—outside just a few minutes ago. He kissed me, and we have a date set for tonight." She held up her finger. "And nothing—not a demon or a warlock—is going to keep me from going on this date."

Phoebe shook her head. "Sounds like Jake has already put a spell on your heart."

Piper held up a finger. "What did I tell you about mentioning love spells ever again?"

Phoebe laughed, and glanced around the Railyard Café. Elena was there in her colorful scarves, doing her tarot readings. She turned her attention to the echoing footsteps and saw Prue. She was smiling brightly, a little bounce in her step.

Prue settled into her seat with a contented sigh.

"What are you so happy about?" Phoebe asked.

"I just got flowers in a Victorian vase with a sweet note from Robert. I sent him an e-mail apologizing for being so rude and blowing him off while he was here."

"Sounds like he's forgiven you," Phoebe said.

"I think so. He's back in Paris but says he may be in the Bay Area in the spring. He wants to take me out for lunch."

"That's wonderful!" Piper said.

Prue leaned forward. "But I promise you both, I'm going to wait a while before I kiss him—or anyone!"

Shaking her head, Phoebe laughed along with Piper. "Yeah, yeah. We've heard that one before."

"I wonder if he ever got the necklace from Claiborne," Prue said.

"If he didn't, it's not our fault," Piper told her. "As soon as Lascaris's spirit was safely inside it, Phoebe and I returned it to Claiborne's house via another time freeze."

"Claiborne never noticed it was missing?" Prue asked.

"Nope," Piper said. "We put it right back where we found it."

"Are you sure you want to go out with Robert?" Phoebe asked, furrowing her brow. "I mean, do you think it's safe now that he's got the necklace?"

"I think it's okay—Lascaris is trapped for another hundred years. Besides, I'm sure Robert doesn't know the emerald is really a prison for a warlock," Prue said.

"At least we *hope* he doesn't know," Phoebe added.

Prue took a sip of water. "To Robert it's a seventeenth-century necklace with a very valuable emerald. He's just an antiques dealer, Phoebe. Like me."

Phoebe raised an eyebrow. "Like you? You're a witch."

Prue sighed. "Good point."

"Pardon me, ladies," Elena said, smiling. "Would you like to have your fortunes told?"

Prue glanced quickly at her sisters before meeting Elena's gaze. "Uh, no, thanks."

Phoebe watched Elena walk away. "That memory-erasing spell worked," she said. "She had no idea who we are."

"Let's keep it that way," Prue suggested. "Her predictions were a little too accurate for my taste."

"True," Piper agreed, thinking of Jake. "I've got to say, I've been noticed lately."

"Wait a minute," Phoebe said, remembering her own fortune. "I didn't even come close to getting any money." Something shiny on the floor caught her eye. Phoebe reached for it, then smiled as she held up a brand-new shiny quarter for her sisters to see. "Well, what do you know . . ."

About the Author

When not working as a computer programmer, Brandon Alexander writes gothic horror and other types of stories for young readers. He enjoys building 3-D puzzles in his spare time and riding the Tower of Terror at Disney World. Brandon has spent most of his life in Texas and currently lives near Dallas.

YOU COULD WIN A DIAMOND HEART PENDANT JUST LIKE PRUE'S!

Cast Your Own Spell—Enter Now!
4 Chances to Win!

1 Grand Prize:
A diamond heart pendant just like the one
Prue wears on the show.
50 First Prizes:
A Charmed baby doll T-shirt.

Enter now!
50 winners who enter from KISS OF DARKNESS will receive
a Charmed baby doll T-shirt. More chances to win
in these upcoming Charmed books.

THE CRIMSON SPELL (April 2000)
WHISPERS FROM THE PAST (June 2000)
VOODOO MOON (August 2000)

Grand prize winner will be chosen from all entries received from sweepstakes in KISS OF DARKNESS,
THE CRIMSON SPELL, WHISPERS FROM THE PAST, and VOODOO MOON combined.
No purchase necessary. See details on back.

Complete entry form and send to:
Pocket Books/ "Charmed Sweepstakes"
1230 Avenue of the Americas, 13th Floor, NY, NY 10020

NAME _____ BIRTHDATE ___/___/___

ADDRESS _____

CITY _____ STATE _____ ZIP _____

PHONE _____

PARENT OR LEGAL GUARDIAN'S SIGNATURE (REQUIRED FOR ENTRANTS UNDER 18 YEARS OF AGE AT TIME OF ENTRY.)

_____

See back for official rules.   **Book Code #C2**

Pocket Books/ "Charmed Sweepstakes"
Sponsors Official Rules:

1. No Purchase Necessary.

2. Enter by mailing this completed Official Entry Form (no copies allowed) or by mailing a 3" x 5" card with your name and address, daytime telephone number, birthdate and parent or legal guardian signature if entrant is under 18 at date of entry to the Pocket Books/ "Charmed Sweepstakes", 1230 Avenue of the Americas, 13th Floor, NY, NY 10020. Entry forms are available in the back of Charmed books KISS OF DARKNESS (2/00) Book Code #C2, THE CRIMSON SPELL (4/00) Book Code #C3, WHISPERS FROM THE PAST (6/00) Book Code #C4 and VOODOO MOON (8/00) Book Code #C5, on in-store book displays and on the web site SimonSays.com. Sweepstakes begins 2/1/00. Please indicate the applicable book code # (i.e. C2, C3, C4 or C5) on your entry form and the envelope. Entries must be postmarked by 8/31/00 and received by 9/15/00. Not responsible for lost, late, damaged, postage-due, stolen, illegible, mutilated, incomplete, or misdirected or not delivered entries or mail or for typographical errors in the entry form or rules or for telecommunication system or computer software or hardware errors or data loss. Entries are void if they are in whole or in part illegible, incomplete or damaged. Enter as often as you wish, but each entry must be mailed separately. Grand prize winner will be selected at random from all eligible entries received. There will be 4 separate drawings for first prize winners and for each such drawing 50 winners will be chosen from all eligible entries received for each of books 2-5 in the Charmed series. Thus there will be 1 drawing for the entries received for KISS OF DARKNESS and 1 drawing for THE CRIMSON SPELL, etc. The drawing for grand prize and first prizes will be held on or about 9/25/00. Winners will be notified by mail. The grand prize winner will be notified by phone as well.

3. Prizes: One Grand Prize: A diamond heart pendant like Prue's (approx. retail value: $500.00). 200 First Prizes: A Charmed baby doll T-shirt (approx. retail value: $8.00 each).

4. The sweepstakes is open to legal residents of the U.S. (excluding Puerto Rico) and Canada (excluding Quebec) ages 12-21 as of 8/31/00, except as set forth below. Proof of age is required to claim prize. Prizes will be awarded to the winner's parent or legal guardian if winner is under 18 years of age. Void wherever prohibited or restricted by law. All federal, state and local laws apply. Simon & Schuster, Inc., Parachute Publishing, Spelling Television Inc. and their respective officers, directors, shareholders, employees, suppliers, parent companies, subsidiaries, affiliates, agencies, sponsors, participating retailers, and persons connected with the use, marketing or conduct of this sweepstakes are not eligible. Family members living in the same household as any of the individuals referred to in the preceding sentence are not eligible.

5. One prize per person or household. Prizes are not transferable and may not be substituted except by sponsors, in the event of prize unavailability, in which case a prize of equal or greater value will be awarded. All prizes will be awarded. The odds of winning a prize depend upon the number of eligible entries received.

6. If a winner is a Canadian resident, then he/she must correctly answer a skill-based question administered by mail.

7. All expenses on receipt and use of prize including federal, state and local taxes are the sole responsibility of the winners. Grand prize winner may be required to execute and return an Affidavit of Eligibility and Publicity Release and all other legal documents which the sweepstakes sponsor may require (including a W-9 tax form) within 15 days of attempted notification or an alternate winner will be selected.

8. Winners or winners' parents or legal guardians on winners' behalf agree to allow use of their names, photographs, likenesses, and entries for any advertising, promotion and publicity purposes without further compensation to or permission from the entrants, except where prohibited by law.

9. Winners or winners' parents or legal guardians, as applicable, agree that Simon & Schuster, Inc., Parachute Publishing and Spelling Television, Inc. and their respective officers, directors, shareholders, employees, suppliers, parent companies, subsidiaries, affiliates, agencies, sponsors, participating retailers, and persons connected with the use, marketing or conduct of this sweepstakes, shall have no responsibility or liability for injuries, losses or damages of any kind in connection with the collection, acceptance or use of the prizes awarded herein, or from participation in this promotion.

10. By participating in this sweepstakes, entrants agree to be bound by these rules and the decisions of the judges and sweepstakes sponsors, which are final in all matters relating to the sweepstakes. Failure to comply with the Official Rules may result in a disqualification of your entry and prohibition of any further participation in this sweepstakes.

11. The first names of the winners will be posted at SimonSays.com (available after 9/31/00) or the names of the winners may be obtained by sending a stamped, self-addressed envelope to Prize Winners, Pocket Books "Charmed Sweepstakes," 1230 Avenue of the Americas, 13th Floor, NY, NY 10020.